Rocky

"Stray Dog Saves Boy's Life"

Book One

By Anne Fox

Illustrations by Elizabeth Jung

This book is dedicated to:

My sister Carlene, because she always believed in me

My son Brian, because I will always believe in him

To all the Emergency Rescuers and their K-9 partners who

train endless hours to perform countless hours of rescues,

and to the lives you have saved

And to my Lord whose grace inspired me

Contents

Introduction

My name is Rocky Rescue. I'm a dog and a very lucky one because I am an official member of an emergency search and rescue team. My human partner is Paramedic Chase Carter. We work for Trinity Emergency Medical Service. Our job is to save lives and to rescue people from all types of dangerous situations.

Flashing red lights and the wail of sirens have probably called your attention to an ambulance, police car, or fire truck rushing to an unknown crisis. Do you ever wonder what kind of emergency is waiting for them? Have you ever watched these heroes in action and wondered what they were doing? Come ride along with Chase and me in our giant 4-wheel drive rescue truck. You will be first on the scene and I will explain what the rescuers are doing and why they do it.

In my first book, I tell you how I became a search and rescue dog, how Chase and I met by "accident", and how we began our many exciting adventures. I hope our stories will interest you in learning first-aid and safety tips that could someday help you to help someone else.

Have a safe day!

Rocky Rescue

Chapter One

Trouble!

Hello! Welcome to the adventures of Rocky Rescue. That's me, you know. I wasn't born with that name and I wasn't always a search and rescue dog. Here's how it all began. When I was a puppy, my name was Trouble. My Dad said I earned it.

I was born in a garage with three sisters and two brothers. We all looked the same except different. We each had white fuzzy legs and white fluffy tummies. The top of our heads and backs looked liked we had walked under a dripping black paint can. Some of the black ran down some of our sides and some of the black just stayed on top. I had a black stripe that ran down my nose. Mom thought it made me look adorable. Our tails curled up and we looked like we were walking around with a furry backward letter C.

Mom and Dad told us that one day we would each move away to live with a new family. We were taught the Four Golden Dog

Rules to live by. Rule #1: Always protect our family from harm. Rule #2: Play gently with the children. Rule #3: Never, never chew on anything that wasn't ours. And Rule #4: Never, never, never relieve ourselves inside the house.

I guess I became the rebel with a cause. 'Cause I didn't want to live with another family and I didn't want to follow any dumb rules!

When we were about six weeks old, different people started showing up at our house. They would look at each of us from nose to tail. My brothers would stand tall and look alert like good watch dogs. My sisters would wag their bodies with their tails and make cutesy little whimpers. Such mush!

I had several ways to keep from being picked. One was to play "Backyard Terror". I would pull the clean clothes off the line and drag them through the mud. Then I would drag out the new garden hose and attempt to chew as many holes in it as possible before feeling a smack on my tail end. Sometimes I would play "Hyper Puppy". In this game, I would jump all over the people, licking their faces, snagging clothes with my claws, and tugging on shoe laces. If all else failed I played "Crazy Mutt". I would run around the back yard chasing and barking at an invisible rabbit. I would growl at a rock, tip over the water bowl, and slobber on the lady. One of these always worked. My parents were always embarrassed and our owner would always say, "That one puppy is nothing but trouble!"

I was the only puppy to get a name before being adopted. Although Trouble is not a name to be proud of, I felt a puppy had to do what a puppy had to do.

One by one, my brothers and sisters left home to live with their new families. The first few days of being the only puppy were great. I got a lot of attention and the food bowl was never crowded. Soon I became bored because there was no one to play with. Dad told me I better start acting right if I wanted to have any kind of a future. I knew he was right, but sometimes it was just so hard to be good.

One spring morning, I was happily chewing on another new laundry basket that I had dragged from the garage when I heard the gate open. I quickly jumped up and tried to hide the mangled 24 inch wide basket behind my 12 inch wide body. With my tail between my legs and the most pitiful puppy look I could muster, I waited for a smack on my tail end. Instead, my owner said, "He's the last of the litter."

A man and lady knelt down and looked me over like I was a toy, and they didn't know where the batteries went.

He said, "He looks good."

She asked, "How big will he get?"

My owner told them I was 6 months old and probably would not get much bigger.

Wrong!

I politely wagged my tail and tried to mind my manners. This was not easy because the lady's purse was slowly swinging in front of my nose. The smell of leather had me drifting off into a daydream of delicious chewing. My dream was abruptly interrupted when the man picked me up and headed to their car.

Good bye Mom. Bye Dad.

I had never been in a car before. This was fun! I ran back and forth across the seat to look out the windows. Everything was going by so fast that I could barely see what I was seeing. We finally arrived at a very large house. They must have a lot of kids to fill such a big home! We went straight inside and I immediately began sniffing every inch. Where were all the children?

I turned a corner and found myself sniffing a strange looking white, furry paw attached to an even stranger looking white, furry animal. It had glowing green eyes and small pointed ears. All of its fur was standing straight up and its back was arched like an upside down horseshoe. This weird creature was making a weird sound like growling and hissing at the same time. How did it do that?

My instincts told me this was a cat. What am I supposed to do with a cat? Let me think. Oh yeah, I chase them! I let out two quick barks to get the cat into the game. This cat didn't want to play and it wasn't running anywhere. It just stood very tall and kept making that strange growling-hissing noise. I wish I could do that. Maybe this cat had never seen a dog before and didn't know how to play the game. I reared back on my haunches and poised to lunge forward. *YIPE!* My nose was suddenly stinging. That fur ball had scratched me and I never even saw its paw move!

My man owner laughed and said, "That will teach you to not mess with Samantha!"

Samantha? What a stupid name for a cat. Dad always said he didn't know why humans gave names to cats. They don't listen and won't come if you call them. You can believe I won't be calling her. Okay, Rule # 1 of my new home, "Don't Mess With The Cat."

The next day I searched that large house for children but never found any. My lady owner kept talking about "when the baby comes". Every day I watched for the mailman and would bark excitedly when he came near the door. Every day he would leave some letters, but never any boxes with a baby. I wish it would hurry and get here; I'm bored!

This house must have some toys somewhere. After searching several rooms, I found a pair of slippers under the bed. I took one to the living room and settled down for a leisurely chew. *Yum!* It was soft on the outside and chewy on the inside. I must have fallen asleep with it in my mouth. I was suddenly awakened by a painful smack on my tail end and the remnants of the slipper being jerked from my mouth. I spent the night outside.

A few days later a noise from the kitchen woke me from a peaceful snooze. I thought everyone was asleep. One of my jobs is to protect the family, plus I was curious, so I went to investigate. Samantha was sitting atop the trash can. She turned, looked at me, hissed, and jumped from her perch. As she went airborne, her back legs gave a kick to the trash can. It toppled over and hit the floor with a thud. The contents tumbled out. Two empty bottles clanked together as they rolled around. A large paper bag began to loudly un-crumple. After the initial shock, I detected a faint smell coming from the remaining garbage. Was that a pork chop? I began digging through the debris inside the trash can and pawing unwanted items out of my way. I had dug so deep that only my tail was sticking out. *Aha! There it is!* This tasted so much better than my dry kibble.

The kitchen light came on and I heard, "Trouble! What are you doing? Look at this mess! Bad dog! Bad, bad dog!"

I slept outside again. Every day it seemed I was earning my name more and more.

I guess my new owners finally had enough one night. They had left me in the house and were gone for a long, long time. Bored, I drank all the water from my bowl. I played "Toss and Fetch" with it for a while. I soon began to feel the need to relieve myself so I ran to the back door and whimpered. No one came. I whimpered louder and scratched. Still no one came and now I really had to go. Finally I could hold it no longer. I ran behind a chair and gave a sigh of relief. I also saw Samantha had been watching from atop the fireplace mantle. *Uh oh.*

Next, the front door opened. Double *uh, oh*!

"What's that smell?" The lady owner asked as she crinkled her nose.

Samantha jumped from the mantle and smugly pranced toward the chair. She began meowing like there was no tomorrow. The man owner went to see what her problem was. His nose led him to the problem.

"Trouble! That's it! Tomorrow you're out of here!"

I slept outside again. *Sigh!*

The next morning I heard my man owner call my name. I ran to the gate and saw him holding my leash. Oh boy! We're either going for a walk or a ride in the car. I love to do both. *Which is it? Which is it?* I danced around and around with excitement. We went out the gate and to the front yard. He opened the car door and I eagerly jumped in.

We went for a long ride – way out in the country. He finally stopped the car next to a field out in the middle of nowhere. He let me out and removed my leash and collar. *What are we doing out here? Are we picking up the new baby?*

He took a steak bone from a plastic bag he had in the car and threw it far out into the field. He yelled, "Go get it!"

Great! We're playing Fetch. This is going to be so much fun! I eagerly ran across the field in search of the bone. I was proud of myself for finding it so quickly. Holding it in my mouth, I began prancing back to my man owner. I saw him get in the car and close the door. I heard the engine start and watched as the car sped away. I began running to catch up.

Wait! I'm not in the car! I'm...not...in...the... The car was gone from sight.

I stood in the middle of the road and waited for him to return. After I became tired of standing, I sat down and waited some more. Maybe he wasn't coming back.

I dropped the bone from my mouth as a very uncomfortable feeling came over me. Did he forget me? Had I really been so bad? How will I get home? I had no idea where I was. These thoughts were disrupted by a rumble in my stomach. I hadn't had breakfast and I was getting hungry. The steak bone did not have any meat left, so I began looking around for something to eat. The field obviously did not have any puppy mix so I started walking down the long road in search of food.

The sun was about to set by the time I saw the first house. The evening air was chilly and my stomach growled from hunger. I sniffed around the house. What luck! I found a large pan filled with chunks like my parents eat. I wolfed down several large bites.

Suddenly from behind me, I heard a *"Woof!"* so loud that it shook the ground. I jumped and turned to face the biggest, meanest dog with the longest, sharpest teeth I had ever seen. I don't think my paws touched the ground as I high tailed it out of there. This monster dog was so close I could feel his hot breath on my tail. One bite and I would have replaced his supper I had just eaten. I shifted my body into turbo drive and ran for my life. After what felt like forever, the monster dog's barking seemed to be getting farther and farther away. Was I just imagining? I took a quick look behind me. He had stopped! He was attached to a long chain that was attached to the house. I gave a big sigh of relief but kept running – just in case.

When my legs became too tired to run anymore, I slowed to a walk. I kept looking back over my shoulder – just in case.

I walked all night and part of the next day before I saw another house. All the windows were broken and the paint was faded and peeling. The front porch was leaning and appeared about to collapse. This old farm house looked sad from being abandoned. I started feeling sad too but shook it off. I sniffed around for big dogs or other surprises but did not find anything. This would be my campground for the night.

The morning sun woke me from a restless sleep. My stomach told me it was time for breakfast so I headed back down that long lonely road. No food was found that day but I did discover a pond and took a long refreshing drink of water. The next few days I ate only a few scraps that I was able to dig out of some garbage bags that had been dumped on the side of the road. My paws were sore and my fur had caught a bushel of stickers.

A few days (or was it weeks?) later I came upon another farm house. The fresh white paint was bright, and cheery yellow curtains danced in and out of the open windows. A rather plump lady was digging in a garden full of colorful vegetables. I approached slowly then cowered when she looked my way. I was so weak that I couldn't have fought or run away if my life depended on it.

"Well, hello Poochie! Another lost stray. When will people learn you don't treat an animal like a bag of trash? C'mon Poochie, I know you must be starving."

I followed her to the house and wondered what she had to eat. My stomach reminded me not to be picky and to just be grateful for any food.

"Now you wait here and I'll be right back." she said as she went in the house. She returned a few minutes later carrying a large bowl with a wonderful smell wafting from whatever was inside. She set the feast down in front of me and the hunger almost made me forget my manners. I told her "Thank you" with my eyes then wolfed down that delicious mix of chicken and dog kibble.

I was miserable again – wonderfully, miserably full. I stretched out on the soft green grass to rest my aching legs and take a nap. The nice lady sat down beside me with a large brush. She stroked my fur and removed all the stickers. I fell asleep thinking how nice it would be to live here.

My sleep was interrupted by the sound of a clunky old blue pickup coming up the drive. A big burly man stepped from the pickup and looked in our direction. "Martha! What's that dog doing here?"

"George," she pleaded, "He was hungry!"

"He's just another stray!" George retorted, "You ain't taking in no more animals. We can't keep up with the ones you already drug in."

"But, George, please? He was starving!"

"No! No! No! And that's final!" George shook his head and muttered under his breath as he went in the house and slammed the door behind him.

Martha slowly turned to me and said, "I'm sorry Poochie. What George says goes, always has, always will. You best be on your way. Take care of yourself."

Oh well, it was nice while it lasted.

The next few weeks (or had it been months?) took me up and down hilly roads and across many fields. Food was scarce and my stomach constantly grumbled from hunger. I slept during the day because at night I had to hide from the coyotes who were also hunting for food. They watched me as if I was a walking hot dog. Once again my fur was matted and full of stickers. My paws were almost raw from the rough terrain. I wish I had a home.

Chapter Two

A Rocky Rescue

One particular day had started out like any other but was soon to change my life forever. I had come to a wooded area with many hills and high cliffs. A small cave looked to be a safe place for me to catch some sleep. As I curled up in my temporary bedroom, I heard tires skidding, rocks falling, and someone screaming. I ran to the top of the hill and managed to stop just in time. The top of the hill abruptly dropped off into a very deep rocky ravine. At the bottom of the ravine I saw a boy about 16 years old and what was left of a bicycle. Apparently he did not know about the sudden drop and was unable to stop his bicycle before they both tumbled to the bottom. The boy was lying on his back and moaning. Blood was covering his head, and his left leg was twisted in the wrong direction. He was in serious trouble.

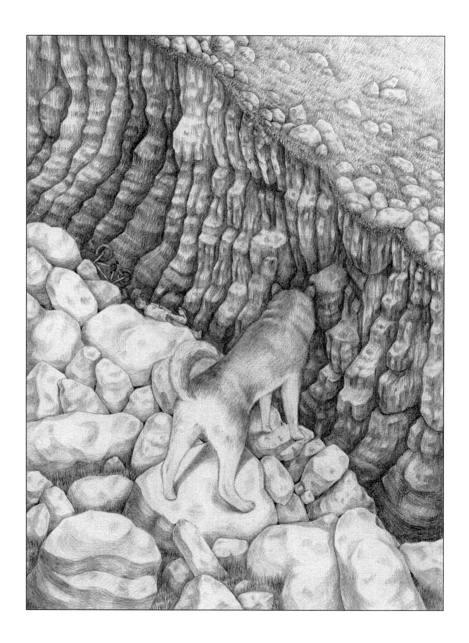

My first instinct was to go help him. I quickly looked for another way down but all four sides were very steep. Sharp rocks jutted out all the way to the ground. I took two steps forward for a better look. Wrong move! The soft ground crumbled beneath my legs. The earth and rocks gave way and I tumbled head over tail to the bottom. After shaking away the stars circling my head, I discovered I had landed next to the boy. I did a head to toe sniff check. He was really hurt. I licked his face to let him know he was not alone.

He barely opened his eyes and moaned, "Help me."

This had to be the most helpless feeling a puppy could have. I'm supposed to protect people and here I stood with a stupid look on my muzzle. This was going to be more than I could handle. I needed human help. Looking around, I wondered how I was going to get out of there. The top of the hill looked a mile away. It wasn't, but it might as well have been. I was just a puppy and wasn't being much help. No, wait; I am NOT a puppy anymore. I am a dog and a dog's got to do what a dog's got to do!

Forgetting about how weak and hungry I was, I lunged toward one side of the cliff wall with all the strength I could muster. I didn't even make it half way up when I lost my footing and somersaulted back to the ground. *Can't give up! Can't give up!* Taking a deep breath, I jumped on the wall and managed to claw my way up. When I reached the top I hit the ground running and kept running.

Finally I found two men at a campsite. Hoping they would understand, I ran to the first man, barked and spun around. "Look at this crazy dog! What are you doing, dancing for your supper? Hey Henry, throw him a hamburger!"

Thanks very much but this is an emergency. Please come with me!

"George, I don't think he's hungry but something sure has him upset," the second camper said as he stood up and walked toward me. I ran a few yards away and began barking and spinning again.

"What is he doing?" asked George.

Henry replied, "Maybe he thinks he's Lassie and wants us to follow him." They both laughed and sat down next to the tent.

No! You've got to come with me!

I ran back to them and began barking louder. Henry stood back up and said, "I can't stand it. Let's see what he wants."

Yes! Yes!

I started running down the road. I looked back and saw George and Henry following in their pickup.

When we came to the cliffs, I ran to the ledge and looked down. The boy was still lying there like a crumpled rag doll. He had lost more blood and now he was not moving. I looked at George and Henry, looked down at the boy, looked back at the men, and barked over and over. The two men got out of the pickup and ran to the edge of the cliff. They looked down and saw the boy.

Henry gasped, "Oh my gosh!"

George ran back to the pickup to grab his cell phone. "I'll call 911 for an ambulance."

Minutes seemed like hours before I heard the wail of sirens. An ambulance and a fire truck were the first to arrive. Two emergency medical technicians and four fire fighters were briefed by George. When the rescuers looked over the edge of the cliff they knew the boy was in serious trouble and immediately tried to find a way down. Recent heavy rains had saturated the surface ground and made it very unstable. Too much movement could cause a mud and rock slide. The ravine was too narrow for a helicopter to fit in, and the walls were too steep for 4-wheelers. The drop to the bottom was about fifty feet.

The rescuers were checking all the sides for a way down when more sirens could be heard in the distance. A few minutes later a police car followed by a very large black truck arrived on the scene. A police officer jumped from his unit and ran to the other rescuers. The big truck reminded me of a big bull. It looked mean and powerful. The engine roared as it climbed up the hill. The body was shiny black with the words "Trinity Search and Rescue" painted in bright red on the doors. The truck had a matching camper shell that was just as high as the roof. All the windows were dark tinted. I counted four or five antennas.

Red and blue emergency lights flashed on the top and in the front and rear lights. The front had a large winch attached to a heavy chromed grill. *Oops!* Someone made a mistake! The word "Paramedic" on the front of the grill was spelled backward! At least they got it right on the back bumper. The monster tires supported all this and made the truck look giant. When the truck came to a stop, a very large man with a dark beard stepped out. He looked like a grizzly bear. I hoped he was friendly. He quickly joined the others and was briefed on the boy.

The police officer said, "Ben, I think that's Chase down there. He's so far down that I can't be sure, but he's wearing the same color clothes that Chase had on this morning when he left for school. The bike is the same color also."

Ben put his large hand on Lt. Carter's shoulder and reassured him, "We'll do everything we can. You know this isn't the first time I've made a call on your boy. He's a pretty tough kid. I'll let you know as soon as I get down there."

Ben got back in the big truck and put it in gear. *Wait! Where are you going? You just said you were going to do everything you could!* I ran to the truck and barked at the tires. I'm not sure what good that would have done, but I couldn't believe he was leaving. I was embarrassed when I saw that he was just moving the truck to a different position. Hey, remember, I didn't know anything about rescues at this time.

The E.M.T.'s were taking equipment out of the ambulance. Ben was fastening some kind of weird looking harness around his pants. He quickly took some heavy ropes with large hooks on each end from the back of the truck. He attached one hook to the back of the truck and the other to the harness. He put on leather gloves and a helmet. Next he looked over the edge. He had moved the truck several yards away so that any rocks that came loose during his climb down would not fall on the boy. That's smart thinking! He slung a large canvas bag over his shoulder and stood backward on the ledge. He put his head down, closed his eyes, and said something very softly. The only thing I heard was "Amen." Checking the ropes one more time, he lowered himself down the cliff. Every few feet several rocks came loose and tumbled to the ground. I could tell he was trying to hurry but he was also being very careful. About half way down, several rocks and large chunks of dirt dislodged beneath his feet. A few more came loose from above his head and struck his helmet. Ben was dangling in mid air for a few seconds before he regained his footing. Finally he made it to the bottom.

Ben quickly unhooked the rope and ran to the boy. He had some kind of tool around his neck that had two tubes on one end and a round metal piece on the other. He put the two tubes in his ears and placed the round piece on the boy's chest. What in the world is he doing? He took a walkie-talkie from his pocket and radioed to the anxious father and rescuers, "He's alive. And, John, it is Chase."

Everyone gave a brief collective sigh of relief. Chase was alive, but for how long? That was a long fall, and he could have numerous internal injuries in addition to the obvious broken leg and head wound. Lt. Carter turned away as he felt the sting of tears in his eyes.

About that time, another car drove up. This was a small blue car that didn't seem to have any emergency equipment. A lady stepped out and ran to Lt. Carter. "John, is that Chase? Is he the one down there?" She was almost hysterical.

Lt. Carter wrapped his arms around his wife and said, "Yes, Laura, it is." He quickly added, "But he's okay. The paramedic is down there with him right now. They'll have him out of there soon." Lt. Carter felt guilty for telling her Chase was okay when he really didn't know. He felt the best thing for her and Chase right now was to get her calmed down. This was one of the times he regretted giving her a police scanner for Christmas.

Earlier that morning the school had called Mrs. Carter and told her Chase had skipped school again. He had left the house angry because she would not let him wear his favorite jeans with all the holes. Chase had a history of being reckless when he was mad. When she heard the call on the scanner about a boy who had been hurt in a bicycle accident, she feared the worse. She had been driving around trying to find Chase and her mother's instinct told her to head that direction.

The couple walked to the cliff's edge and watched Ben tend to their son. I watched with curiosity and ended up with more questions than answers. The paramedic took something out of his bag. It looked like the biggest dog collar I had ever seen. He placed it around Chase's neck. That boy didn't need a dog collar, he's wasn't going anywhere! Next he wrapped some kind of cloth around his head and covered the bleeding wound. He took a green colored tank out of his bag and attached a clear tube to one end. The other end was attached to a clear small mask. He placed the mask over Chase's mouth and nose. Was he giving him laughing gas? *Humph!* I didn't think this was any laughing matter.

Ben used a pair of scissors to cut away Chase's shirt and jeans. His mother is going to be mad! My doggy vision allowed me to see better than the humans. I could see a large bruise on the boy's left side. That's got to hurt! The next action still makes me wince to think about it. He took some kind of metal contraption with short black straps out of his bag and laid it next to Chase's twisted leg. I couldn't believe my eyes. He was pulling on that leg! Good grief! What is he doing to that poor boy? I looked around at the other people to see if they were going to stop this insanity. No one seemed upset or alarmed. Maybe they knew something I didn't. I hope so! Ben gently placed the now straight leg in the contraption and fastened the straps.

Ben radioed the E.M.T.'s and told them to send down a back-board and basket.

Basket? Is he going to take time for lunch? The E.M.T.'s attached ropes to a long board that looked sort of like a surf board without the fin and lowered it to Ben. The next thing they sent down must have been the basket he requested. It was a little bit longer than the back board and made of metal mesh. Ben carefully rolled Chase onto his side and then rolled him on to the back board. He used long wide strips of cloth to secure his head, arms and legs to the board. He then lifted the board with Chase and gently set both inside the basket. He's strong! The paramedic took long straps with buckles that looked like they were for seatbelts and attached them around the basket. The firefighters sent down four more ropes with hooks on the ends. Ben attached a hook to the four corners of the basket. He gave a "thumbs up" to the rescuers at the top.

In unison, each rescuer slowly pulled on their end of the ropes. Chase was finally on his way out of the ravine. When the precious cargo reached the top, the firefighters lifted Chase out of the basket and placed him on a bed with wheels that the E.M.T.'s had taken from the back of the ambulance. Lt. Carter and Laura rushed to their boy.

"Chase! Chase! Are you okay?" his nervous mother asked.

Chase barely opened his eyes and murmured, "Wobby wehgoo."

His dad asked, "What, Chase? What are you trying to say?"

Chase again murmured, "Wobby wehgoo."

No one could understand what he was trying to say. Laura said they could figure it out later; right now he needed to get the hospital. Ben had made it back to the top and helped the E.M.T.'s load Chase into the ambulance. Ben told the E.M.T.'s he would meet them at the Emergency Room. The ambulance sped away with lights and siren.

John and Laura thanked Ben for saving their son's life. They then turned to George and Henry to thank them. Henry said, "Don't thank us. Thank your dog. If he hadn't found us, there is no telling when your boy would have been rescued."

Laura asked, "What dog?"

George and Henry pointed to me.

"That's not our dog. He must be a stray, look how skinny and shaggy he is," Lt. Carter replied.

Mrs. Carter walked over, patted me on the head and said, "Thank you, thank you for saving my son."

What a nice lady!

George and Henry said they would stop by the hospital later to check on Chase. They got back in their pickup and left. Laura told her husband she would meet him at the hospital and left in her car. Lt. Carter helped the fire fighters and Ben load the rest of the rescue equipment back into the big truck. The fire truck and giant rescue truck also left. Lt. Carter walked toward his police car and was ready to head to the hospital.

Wow! This had certainly been an exciting day. It was amazing to watch the rescuers work together to save Chase. They must go through a lot of training. Ben must be the smartest, bravest, and strongest man I have ever seen. Chase sure was lucky to have parents who loved him so much. I wish I could live with a family like the Carters. Oh well, I guess it's time to move on. I was really hungry after all this. As I walked away I heard someone whistle.

Chapter Three

Home At Last

I turned around to see Lt. Carter standing next to his police car with the back door open. He whistled again and called, "C'mon boy! You didn't think I'd leave behind our hero?"

Hero? Who, me? Wow! I've been called a lot of things but never a hero. My parents would sure be proud!

"Chase has wanted a dog and I can't think of a single one better suited than you. Would you like a home?"

A home? Live with the Carters? *Yes! Yes! Yes!* My tail wagged my whole body as I eagerly jumped into the back seat.

It was fun riding in a police car. Lt. Carter rolled down the back window so I could stick my head out. I got a lot of looks from people in other cars. I pretended to be a police dog and was on the look-out for bad guys.

A few miles later we drove into a neighborhood. The streets were lined with trees, flowers bloomed around porches, and I took in the wonderful smell of freshly cut grass. We pulled into the driveway of a tan brick house. The trim was painted blue and a small wood plaque next to the front door said, "Welcome friends". Lt. Carter opened the car door and led me to the back yard. This was just as nice as the front yard. The grass was soft and green. Two big pecan trees provided lots of shade.

Lt. Carter said, "I'll be right back." He went in the house and returned a few minutes later carrying two large bowls. He set them down in front of me. "This will have to do for now. I've got to get the hospital to check on Chase; then I'll pick up some dog food for you. Make yourself at home".

One bowl was filled with fresh water and the other with roast beef. I emptied both in record time. *Yum! Yawn!* Now a nap was needed. I stretched out beneath one of the trees and thought about the events of the day. I hoped Chase was going to be okay. I wondered what it would be like to be a real rescuer. I thought about Mrs. Carter thanking me and Lt. Carter calling me a hero. I realized I had a new family. I am home!

All this thinking made me sleepy. I was just about to doze off when I felt something flick my nose. I raised my head but didn't see anything. I had barely closed my eyes when something flicked my nose again. *All right, who's the wise guy?* I jumped up to catch the culprit but did not see anyone. I heard muffled laughter coming from above. Looking up I saw two cats sitting on a branch. One had a small twig in her mouth and was poised directly over my head. *Oh no!* Now I have to deal with two feline delinquents!

The two cats scurried down the tree and came over to meet me. The first one, a gray and white striped tabby, purred and rubbed her head under my chin. The second, an orange, black, and white calico, was a bit stand-offish. She sniffed me from a distance then walked away with no further interest. She went to the house and through a small door in the larger door. Now that's cool! I had heard of pet doors but had never seen one. I had to check this out. I went to the pet door and stuck my head in. I could see the kitchen and a bowl of some kind of food on the floor. It smelled like fish so it was probably cat food. I've never had cat food and thought I'd give it a try. There was only one problem. The rest of me would not fit through that little door. I tried to back out but found I was stuck. Now why is it my big head would fit going in but not coming out? I pulled again but no luck. Now what am I going to do? Great, the first day in my new home and I'm already in trouble. I braced my front paws against the outside of the pet door and used my back legs to pull. I pulled and pulled. Nope, I was stuck. The calico came into the kitchen, saw my predicament, and rolled on the floor laughing. *This isn't funny. Help me out of here!* Well she helped all right. She walked back and forth under my nose allowing her tail to barely brush my whiskers. *Stop it! That tickles!* To make matters worse the tabby, still on the outside, decided to play "Swat the Dog's Tail". How humiliating! I'm trapped and at the mercy of cats. The calico kept running her tail under my nose until I started sneezing. *Achoo! Achoo! Achoo!* Three good sneezes and my head popped back out the door. *Whew!*

Just a few minutes later the back door opened and I saw Mrs. Carter. She said, "Here boy!" and handed me a large raw hide bone. *Yum!* "This is just a little something to say thank you again for saving Chase's life today. He was very lucky that you came along. I've told him all about you and he can't wait to come home. The doctor said it would be a few weeks. Well, I just came home to give you the bone and pick up a few things for Chase. I'm going back to the hospital – have a good evening!"

I began a leisurely chew on the bone and thought about how nice she was. She even talked to me like I was a person. How about that!

The next morning I was invited into the house. If I had known the invitation was for a bath, I would have respectfully declined. Afterward, I went outside and tried to shake away all the wet clean smell. I rolled in the grass and shook some more. The smell of flowery shampoo was not going away. If I had any dog friends, they sure would be making fun of me. I hated to admit it, but I did feel better.

That afternoon, I was invited inside again. *No thank you. The back yard suits me just fine.*

"C'mon boy. We've got a surprise for you." Lt. Carter coaxed.

I hoped these people weren't some kind of clean-freaks. One bath is really about all I can handle. I cautiously went inside. Mrs. Carter was standing at the end of the hall and calling for me. *Oh no you don't! The bathtub is down there!* She called again and assured me that I wasn't going to get another bath. I decided to trust her and low crawled down the hall. Now I noticed she was standing next to another room and not the bathroom. I looked in and saw a human bed. On the floor next to it was a large round pillow inside a large wicker basket. "You're going to share Chase's room. We know he'll want you nearby when he comes home."

I stepped into the basket and my paws sunk into the softness of the pillow. Oh, that felt wonderful! *If it's alright with everyone, I think I'll take a little nap.* I curled up and settled in for a peaceful snooze.

"K.C. ! Leave him alone!" The sudden noise woke me to see a gray striped paw hovering about two inches above my nose. K.C. quickly withdrew her paw to her mouth and pretended to be cleaning it. What was she about to do?

During the next few weeks I learned a lot about the two cats that shared my new home. K.C. (which is short for Kitty Cat) is the gray and white striped tabby. She's the practical joker of the pair. The other day she was sitting on a low tree branch that hung over the fence separating the back from the front yard. She was staring up at the sky as if intently watching something. I didn't see anything. A little boy came by and looked up to see what the cat was watching. A few minutes later a man came by and looked up to see what the cat and the little boy were watching. Next a lady came by and she also looked up. Two little girls walked by and joined the group of watchers. K.C. apparently thought she had gathered a large enough crowd and quietly climbed down. She casually walked to the porch then turned to watch the fun. When another lady walked by she looked at the group and looked up to see what they were watching. She was the first to ask what everyone was looking at. One person said they were trying to see what the cat was staring at. This lady looked around and asked, "What cat?" The little boy pointed to the empty tree branch. Everyone looked at each other with a puzzled expression, shook their heads, and walked away. K.C. was rolling on the ground with laughter.

Cally is the other cat. She is white with big black and orange spots. She is not as mischievous as K.C. but can be easily talked into assisting with a prank. A good example of this happened one morning. I was sprawled out on the couch with my head resting on the arm. Cally was sitting on the back of the recliner and watching birds outside the window. K.C. was batting a rubber ball in the bath tub. You could hear *Bap! Thump, thump, thump. Bap! Thump, thump, thump.*

Mrs. Carter was dressed in faded blue jeans and one of Lt. Carter's old t-shirts. Her hair was loosely pinned on top of her head and she had black smears on her face from cleaning the oven. The door bell rang and she answered it to find her two snooty friends. They always dropped by unannounced and usually at the worse time. These two ladies did not believe animals should be allowed in the house, they never thought anyone's home was clean enough, and they were appalled at Mrs. Carter's unkempt appearance. Mrs. Carter apologized for the mess then quickly scooped up the two cats and called me to follow. The three of us were put outside. This was fine with me. I didn't like those two.

Cally and K.C. did not take it as well. They sat on the back porch angrily switching their tails. Suddenly they both took off running across the back yard, over the fence, and disappeared down the alley. A few minutes later the pair came back over the fence. Each was carrying a live mouse in their teeth and they were headed to the pet door. *Oh no!* Surely they wouldn't...they can't be going to...oh my gosh, they are! They raced through the pet door and into the house. A moment later I heard screams and saw K.C. and Cally high tailing back out the door, across the yard, and over the fence. I heard the front door slam shut and a car quickly leave. Mrs. Carter opened the back door and used a broom to chase out the frightened but otherwise unharmed mice.

I felt my upper lip curl and felt the almost overwhelming need to burst out laughing. Mrs. Carter sat on the steps and buried her head in her hands. Was she crying? Now I felt bad, even though I had nothing to do with this prank. I went to her and placed my head on her lap. I wanted to apologize for those two ornery felines. She raised her head and I saw that she wasn't crying after all. She was laughing!

"Where are those two knuckleheads? I owe them a big thanks!" She continued laughing as she went back inside.

You see why I love this place?

I kept up with Chase's progress at the hospital by listening to his Mom and Dad. He had a concussion, two broken ribs, and a badly broken leg that required surgery to repair. The main concern was the concussion. I found out this means a large bruise on the brain that causes swelling. Chase lost consciousness for a while but was doing better. The doctor said he was very lucky, especially considering how far he fell. His mother said God must have sent an angel to take care of him. She smiled at me when she said that.

One morning I heard Lt. Carter talking to someone on the phone. He said Chase would be coming home that afternoon. He also said Chase was still really sore and would have to go through a lot of physical therapy.

Oh boy! Chase is finally coming home! I couldn't wait to meet him. Well, actually I mean to meet him again. My thoughts wandered back to the day I saw him at the bottom of that rocky ravine. I remembered how injured he was and how desperate

I was to get him help. I thought about Ben and the other res-cuers. They were so brave and worked so hard to save him. Then I wondered if Chase would like me. What if I'm not the kind of dog he wanted? What if he wanted a monkey or a bird instead? What if I get in trouble and he won't want me anymore? What if... *Okay, dog, shut up and quit thinking about yourself.* I had to remind myself that this wasn't about me. This was about Chase and helping him get better.

Chapter Four

Boy Meets Dog

It seemed like hours had passed since the Carter's left for the hospital. I impatiently waited at the gate to hear their car coming down the road. I waited and waited. I paced around the back yard. I waited some more.

Finally! I recognized the sound of their car engine. I watched the car pull into the drive way. First Mrs. Carter stepped out. Next Lt. Carter got out and opened the trunk. He took out a chair on wheels and set it by the rear door. Mrs. Carter opened the door and I saw him. He was tall and lanky with blond hair and green eyes. A bandage was on his forehead and his left leg was in a hard cast. Lt. Carter held the chair steady while Mrs. Carter helped Chase sit down. He winced in pain as he moved. His dad started to wheel the chair to the house when Chase told him, "Wait."

Chase looked in my direction. We stared at each other for what seemed like a long time. Chase's pained expression turned into a huge smile and I knew he had accepted me. His father said, "Let's get you inside and then you can meet him."

A few minutes later, Mrs. Carter opened the back door and called me. She didn't have to ask twice as I ran into the house. My first instinct was to rush over to Chase and give him a thousand "Hello!" licks. I quickly reminded myself that he had just been released from the hospital and I needed to be easy. So I trotted up, placed my head on his lap, and gently licked his hand. He leaned forward, gave me a warm hug then kissed me on the head. Can you imagine that?

"Hello, Rocky," he said to me.

Rocky?

"Rocky?" his parents asked.

"Rocky Rescue. That's what I've named him."

"Where did you get that name?" his father asked.

"After the accident," Chase explained, "When Ben was taking care of me, he kept talking to me. I had no idea what he was saying. The only thing I remember was him saying something about a rocky rescue. I managed to open my eyes for just a moment. I was looking up the cliff and saw Rocky looking back down at me. For some reason those two words, rocky rescue, kept going around in my head."

"So, that's what you were saying when the E.M.T.'s were loading you into the ambulance!" Mrs. Carter exclaimed. "You kept mumbling something over and over but no one could understand what it was. Now we know. Okay, Rocky Rescue it is!"

We heard a car pull into the driveway followed by the loud rumble of another vehicle. It was Ben and a reporter from the local newspaper. The reporter was going to write a story about Chase and the rescue.

"Hi, Ben!" Chase greeted his hero. "Meet Rocky Rescue."

"We met at the accident," Ben said as he scratched my head. "Where did you come up with that name?"

Chase explained while the reporter took notes. He took several pictures of Chase, Ben, and me.

Chase thanked Ben for saving his life. Ben replied, "I was just doing what I trained for and what I love to do. The real thanks should go to Rocky because you probably could not have lasted very long without help. I'm still amazed that he knew you were in trouble and knew to get help. You're very lucky he came along."

"Yes, I am. He is very special."

What could I say? A dog has to do what a dog has to do.

Chase and I spent the rest of the day getting to know each other. He told me that when he was well we would do all kind of fun things. I liked fun! He said he would let me meet all his friends, we would play ball in the park, we would swim in the lake, and we would race over the hills in the Wichita National Park. *Wait a minute, isn't that where you crashed and burned? Let's think about that one!*

The next morning Mrs. Carter brought the newspaper to Chase. The headline read, "Stray Dog Saves Boy's Life". Chase began reading the article out loud. My mind drifted over the words "stray dog". I remembered other people calling me a stray. My parents never mentioned what breed of dog we were. Well, if people who don't even know me say I'm a Stray and it is printed in the newspaper, then it must be true. Right? So I guess I'm a Stray. I wondered where the breed of Strays came from. Maybe thousands of years ago we were raised as brave watch dogs to guard kings' treasures. Maybe we were trained to fight next to soldiers in famous battles. At any rate, we must be a popular breed because so many people knew what I was as soon as they saw me.

Chase made many more trips to the doctor. About six weeks after the accident the cast on his leg was removed. Now he had to start physical therapy to build the strength back in his muscles. Three days a week he went for exercise sessions. Chase grew impatient with the slow progress of healing. He still had to use crutches because the pain and muscle weakness kept him from supporting much weight on his left leg. He was particularly frus-trated one day after returning from therapy. He hobbled through the front door and tried to take off his jacket while balancing on one leg and one crutch. He lost his balance and fell flat on the floor. Chase sat up and yelled, "Hackity! Hackity! Hackity!"

"Hackity", I learned, was a non-word created by Chase. He once had a problem of using foul language and was often punished. One of his teachers suggested he come up with a replacement for the bad words. So far it's worked. Unfortunately, he still needed to work on his temper.

Chase grabbed one of his crutches and threw it across the living room. The rubber tipped end hit a wall, bounced off and clobbered a lamp, then bonked me on the head. *Yelp!* Chase immediately regained control and reached out to hug me. "Oh, man, I'm sorry, Rocky! Are you okay? I am so sorry!"

I'm okay but you need to learn to chill. I licked his face to let him know all was forgiven. We were best friends and this incident was soon forgotten.

Everyday some of Chase's friends brought his school work home. Chase had missed a lot of school because of the accident and was trying to catch up. His parents were especially concerned because his grades had not been that great and he had been caught skipping school several times. One of those times was the day of the accident.

Ben stopped by about once a week to check on Chase. We loved listening to the stories about his many rescues. A couple of times Ben had come close to losing his own life while trying to save someone else's. *Wow!* He IS brave! Chase would ask a hundred questions about the "what and whys" of being a rescuer. Ben always had the answers. Ben also told Chase that working in the field of emergency medicine required a lot of training and a lot of self discipline. Chase was still working on that second part.

Chase became more determined to get well. He worked harder during physical therapy and was more diligent about the strength training exercises at home. We took walks every day for a while then slowly began jogging as his leg healed. After he had completed the P.T., he continued to work out at home on the weight bench his parents bought for his birthday. In a few months he was in better shape than he was before the accident. He was back in school and had not skipped any more days. *Way to go!* His parents were proud that his grades had improved. "I think my boy is finally growing up", Mrs. Carter remarked after seeing a really good report card.

Chase was also ready to get his driver's license, so his dad decided to teach him. They let me ride in the back seat on his first attempt. I won't do that again! He took out the mail box, a neighbor's flowerbed, and stalled the car in the middle of a very busy intersection. *Please! Just take me home. I'll never ask to ride in the car again!* After many practice drives and his father's frazzled nerves healed, Chase was ready to take the test. Mrs. Carter was worried that he would pass. "He's just not ready for that responsibility."

"We've got to let him grow up," his dad responded. "But I'll make sure our insurance is up to date."

To the surprise of everyone, Chase passed the first time he took the test. Chase ran into his house proudly waving his new driver's license. "Mom! I passed! I can drive all by myself! Can I borrow the car to go to school tomorrow?"

His mother just moaned.

Chase was stopped twice for speeding the first month after he got his license. The third time he was caught by his own father who was running radar in a school zone. It only took one warning that he would take Chase's license away for 6 weeks to cure his heavy foot.

I eventually felt confident enough in Chase's driving skills to get back in a car with him. On the weekends we would go to Trinity Emergency Medical Service and hang out with the crews. Chase helped clean the ambulances and restock the emergency medical supplies. This wasn't work – it was fun. The best part was cleaning and polishing Ben's big rig. Chase often talked to Ben about becoming an Emergency Medical Technician. He was learning a lot from the E.M.T.'s and was thinking seriously about making this his career. Ben was very encouraging and suggested he talk it over with his parents.

Lt. Carter was at first disappointed that his son did not want to follow in his footsteps and become a police officer. His mother was hoping he would choose a safe indoor job. But they both knew he had to follow his heart and were ultimately proud of his decision.

Summer break went by in a hurry. Chase and I had so much fun. He took me everywhere. When we weren't hanging out at the ambulance barn we were playing football with his friends (I was the ball fetcher), flirting with girls (I was the conversation starter), or grabbing a hamburger at the drive-in (I was the taste-tester). All too soon, fall was approaching. Chase was set to begin his senior year of high school. I was sad that we wouldn't be able to spend as much time together, but I knew a boy had to do what a boy had to do.

A few weeks before school started, Ben approached Chase with some exciting information. He said that the community college was going to offer a few courses to seniors if their grades were high enough. Some of the classes would help Chase if he wanted to continue studying Emergency Medicine in college after he graduated from high school. Chase jumped at the chance and was thankful he had brought up his grades. His parents were proud that he was taking his future seriously.

Let the training begin!

Chapter Five

Mummy Dog

C hase began his senior year with new enthusiasm. He now viewed school as a path to his dream instead of endless hours of boredom. He also was accepted into the senior program at the local community college. Each semester he would attend a class three days a week. The first semester class was Anatomy and Physiology.

Explain something to me. How does a class on An Aunt of Me and Fizzy Ollogee prepare a human to become an E.M.T.? I could not go because I don't know any of my aunts. And I already know what happens when you shake a can of soda then pop the top. *Oh, duh!* Chase told me it is the study of the human body and how it functions. Why didn't they say that? *Whew!* I'm glad I'm not taking that class!

Chase brought home his book and studied all the parts of the body. I never realized humans were so complicated. Did you know the human body has over 200 bones? And I don't under-stand why they can't just call them Bone #1, Bone #2, and so on. The jaw bone is called the mandible, the collarbone is the clavicle, and the bone between the shoulder and the elbow is the humerus. I've heard this called the funny bone but it sure isn't funny if you hit it. The leg has three big bones, the femur, the tibia, and the fibula. Then there is a whole bunch of names for all the other little bones. Personally I still prefer steak bones.

I learned that humans have over 600 muscles. Where do they put all this stuff? They have ligaments that connect bones together and tendons that connect muscles to bones. I'm glad to just be a dog. I have a head, a tummy, a tail, and four legs. That's all I need.

I guess breathing is a pretty big deal because they wrote an entire chapter about it. This is another complex system that involves more than just the nose. It also includes the lungs and a bunch of other parts I can't pronounce. Humans have to breathe to live. I wondered if that was true for dogs so I held my breath for a very long time. It wasn't long before I almost passed out. I started gasping for air and thought I was going to suck all the oxygen out of the room before I could catch my breath again. Yep, I can honestly say that breathing is important for dogs, too.

The heart is another big deal. It garnered two chapters. The heart has many parts as a smoker has reasons to quit. The heart pumps blood throughout the body. If it stops, the body stops. I decided to take for granted that a beating heart is important to dogs. No more experiments for me!

Chase learned about the functions of the three major layers of skin. Overall, skin does a lot of things, including: protection from bumps, keeping moisture in or out, keeping germs out, and regulating temperature.

The head, or skull, protects the brain. The brain is very complicated. I couldn't understand anything Chase was saying when he was studying out loud. Thinking about all that made my brain hurt.

The final exam for this course was going to be tough. Chase made flash cards to help him study. On one side of the card he wrote the medical term for a body part. On the other side he wrote its common name and function. He would look at one side and see if he knew what the other side was. Occasionally he would have a brain freeze. "Hackity!" Why can't I remember that meta*carp*al is hand and meta*tars*al is foot?" Chase moaned.

To me a paw is a paw is a paw. Simple.

After weeks of intense studying, Chase passed the first course on his way to a new career. Good work!

His second semester course was called "First Responder". A first responder is the first person to arrive at the scene of an emergency. They provide basic first aid and life saving measures until the ambulance arrives. They also keep the scene free of onlookers who might get in the way of the rescuers. Many police officers and fire fighters take First Responder training.

The first thing Chase learned was to determine if the emergency scene is safe to approach. On T.V. they show the ambulance rushing up to a scene and the E.M.T.'s jumping out and running to the victim. This could be dangerous. At a car accident, gasoline could have leaked onto the ground. A spark could cause a fire or explosion. If the car hit a utility pole there could be downed power lines. A house that has caught fire could be structurally weak and might collapse on the rescuers. Fires can also produce deadly fumes. What about a call on a person who has been shot? Is the suspect still in the area? He might want to ensure the person doesn't get help or that he doesn't get caught. These are just some of the things a rescuer should think about before entering a scene. Always play it safe!

The second thing he learned was how to take care of life threatening emergencies first. This is checking the A.B.C.'s. No, it's not seeing if the victim knows the alphabet. This means to check Airway, Breathing, and Circulation. The airway (such as nose, mouth, and throat) must be free of any obstruction so air can get to the lungs. If the victim is not breathing, the rescuer provides artificial breathing by mouth-to-mouth or with a mask and bag attached to an oxygen tank. The rescuer squeezes the bag which sends oxygen into the victim. He must also check for circulation. This means he checks to see if the victim's heart is beating. If it isn't, the rescuer will perform C.P.R. (Cardiopulmonary Resuscitation).

Another important task, especially if the victim has been involved in an accident, is to protect the neck and spine. The brain tells the body what to do by sending messages through the nerves. This includes telling the lungs to breathe, the heart to beat, legs to move, and fingers to scratch an itch. That reminds me. I had an itch somewhere. Was it on my tummy? Scritch! Scritch! No, that's not it. Maybe it was behind my ear. Scritch! Scritch! Scritch! No, that's not it either. Oh well, it will come to me later. Anyway, these messages are sent from the brain, down the nerves in the spinal cord, and to the other areas of the body. Sometimes if the spinal cord is injured, the nerves become damaged and the brain's messages can't get through. Think about a telephone cord being cut. Since ambulances don't carry x-ray machines, the rescuer can't tell for sure if there is injury. Precautions are taken to stabilize and protect the neck and spine until the victim can be taken to the hospital for x-rays. One piece of equipment used for this is called a cervical collar, or C-collar. A C-collar? That's what Ben placed around Chase's neck that I thought was a huge dog collar. And the long board he placed Chase on is called a back board or spine board. It all makes sense now. Well, at least some of it makes sense. I still had a lot to learn.

Chase had to learn how to bandage wounds and splint broken bones. He needed a volunteer. *Who me? I don't think so. Aw, come on! Use one of the cats as your victim!* Even I didn't think using a cat was a good idea. Oh well, a dog's gotta do what a dog's gotta do.

"Okay, Rocky, let's pretend you have a cut here and here, a broken leg, a sprained shoulder, and let's see ..."

I have what and what? I don't think I want to do this.

First he decided to splint my tail. He placed a board against it and then wound gauze wrap around until only the tip was sticking out. He next splinted my left back leg and put my right front leg in a sling. My body became covered in bandages that were held in place with more gauze wrap. Chase even wrapped my head! At least he left out my eyes and nose.

After completing his handiwork, Chase sat back, looked me over, and laughed hysterically. "We've got to show you to Mom."

I don't think so. Can I get out of this stuff?

"C'mon, Rocky!" Chase walked out of the bedroom and was holding his stomach from laughing so hard. I followed. Well, I tried to follow. It was very difficult to walk. I saw Cally sleeping on the floor in the middle of the hallway, and I knew K.C. wouldn't be far away.

Oh, I hoped those two would not see me like this. I would never hear the end of it!

I slowly eased around the sleeping Cally. My attempt to maneuver around her failed. I lost my balance and of all the places to fall, it had to be on the cat. Cally jumped straight up in the air and turned to see what had assaulted her. She looked at me with terror in her eyes, arched her back, fur puffed out, and began hissing and spitting. Needless to say, all this commotion brought K.C. running. I had managed to get back up on three legs and tried to make my escape. The gauze wrapping was coming loose and falling across my eyes. I could barely see where I was going. A strand from my body was trailing behind me. K.C. saw the wiggly threads and began a pursuit. She pounced and grabbed the end about the same time I was trying to get around the corner. I was jerked backward and tumbled into the coffee table. K.C. tried to run away with her end of the gauze by jumping over the table. I guess she didn't realize it was still attached to me. She did a somersault across the table but refused to let go of the strand. That same strand pulled everything onto the floor. The worse casualty was a glass vase that Mrs. Carter had just filled with fresh flowers. It smashed into a gazillion pieces. The flowers were shredded. Water ran all over the floor.

Uh oh!

K.C. took one look at the disaster, quickly dropped the gauze, and ran to some unknown hiding place. As typical, she left me to take the blame. Mrs. Carter and Chase rushed in to survey the damage. "Oh no!" she cried, "My favorite vase! That belonged to your great-great grandmother. We have too many animals!"

I just lied down and gave a sad puppy look. I'm in trouble now!

Chase quickly came to my defense and told his mother it was his idea for me to come out of the bedroom. He apologized and offered to pay for the vase out of his allowance.

"No," she replied, "This was an accident, even if it was an avoidable one. Next time, please leave your projects in a safe place."

The rest of the day Chase studied his books quietly in his bedroom. I took a long nap under the bed. K.C. and Cally went about as if nothing had happened and, if it had, it certainly wasn't their fault.

Chase learned how to do a Patient Assessment which is checking the victim from head to toe for injuries or problems. The students practiced on each other how to safely lift so they would not cause more injury to the patient or themselves. Yep, you sure don't want to drop someone. Chase had an easier time studying for this test. I think it's because he found it to be more interesting. I can't say the same. I had my fill of being the patient; next time will be the cats' turn.

Chapter Six

He Was Drunk

Chase's high school graduation was just a week away. His hard work had paid off and his good grades made his parents proud. And what would graduation be without a party? Some of his friends planned a big bash on one of their grandfather's farms. He said they could have it in the barn as long as there was no drinking, no drugs, and no fights. Everyone promised the party would stay "mellow".

After the graduation ceremony, Chase traded his cap and gown for blue jeans and his favorite t-shirt. He hoped Amanda Skyler would be at the party, and more important, she would not be with a date. He was anxious to drop his parents off at home so he could head to the farm. Chase pulled in the drive and sat there with the engine running. His mother asked him to come inside for a minute. "Aw, Mom! I'm going to be late!" Chase complained.

His dad responded, "This won't take long. Go inside like your mother said."

Chase grumbled, "Hackity!" under his breath. This was probably going to be a lecture about smoking, drinking, and drugs. He had heard it all before. Chase had his fair share of getting in trouble but he never became involved in any of that. Lt. Carter told his son to follow him to the garage. "Now what?" Chase moaned.

Lt. Carter turned on the garage light that illuminated a shiny red short bed, step side pickup. The sporty chrome wheels glistened. Chase was speechless. *I knew about this all along but I didn't give up the secret.* "This is your graduation present. It's not new, but your Mom and I thought it would a good and reliable truck to start out."

"Wow!" Chase was awestruck as he walked around his new prize. "Wow!" was all he could say.

"So, you like it?" his mother asked.

"Oh my gosh! I love it! Thank you! Thank you so much!" Chase said as he hugged his parents. He started the engine and listened to it purr. "Hey, Rocky! You ready to party?"

You betcha! I jumped through the passenger side open window. *Wow!* I didn't know I could do that!

Chase couldn't wait to show off his new truck as we drove to the barn party. When we arrived, a lot of kids were already there. Chase gathered his friends and began his bragging rights.

He noticed Amanda was standing with the group and did not appear to have a date. Chase seemed to be a bit shy so I decided to help him out. I went up to Amanda, placed my paw on her leg, and gave the most adorable doggy look I could come up with. "Hi, there! Aren't you a cute dog? Who do you belong to?" She asked while petting my head.

Okay, Chase, it's your move.

"That's Rocky Rescue. He's mine. Do you like dogs?"

"I love them. I have two Dachunds."

Tell her I'm a Stray. Go ahead, tell her.

Chase's next words were interrupted by Darren Wilks, the school's star football player. "Hey Amanda, you're looking really good tonight. We're going to blow this place and go to Jason's. His parents are out of town and he's throwing a <u>real</u> party. Wanna come?"

Amanda thought she smelled beer on his breath but ignored it. After all, Darren was the hottest guy at school. She heard he had just broken up with Heather Brock, a cheerleader. She wasn't going to pass up this opportunity. Chase watched as she got into Darren's expensive yellow sports car. "I can't compete with that," Chase sighed. "C'mon Rocky, let's see what's happening inside. Chase and I started walking to the barn.

Just a moment later we heard the sound of screeching tires then a loud crunch. A minute later a car raced up with its horn blasting. It was Tyler Smith, a friend of Chase's. Everyone ran out of the barn to see what was going on. Tyler was frantic. "There's a really bad crash down there! Two people were thrown out of the car. I think it's Darren's car. They need an ambulance!"

Kids grabbed their cell phones to make the 911 call. Chase and I jumped in his pickup and rushed to the scene. Several other cars filled with kids pulled up behind us. The yellow sports car looked like a soda can that had been crushed against a tree. Amanda was sitting on the ground and holding her right arm. Blood was trickling down her face. Darren was a few feet away lying face up in the middle of the road. He wasn't moving.

Chase stood silent, overwhelmed by the sight. He had just talked to them. How could this happen so fast? I nudged Chase. *Hey! You know first aid. Do something!* Chase gathered his wits and went first to Darren. Amanda was okay at least for now. She was breathing and conscious. Chase kneeled down by the boy. "Darren, are you okay? Darren, can you hear me?" Chase watched his chest rise up and down. *Okay, he's breathing.* Chase looked him over and saw some blood on his shirt. Chase opened his shirt and almost fell backward at the sight. The car's broken turn signal lever was sticking out of his chest. A crowd had gathered and some of the girls screamed when they saw Darren.

"Can I help?" Tyler asked.

"What can I do?" Steve Sanders, another one of Chase's friends inquired.

"Tyler, come over here. I need you to stabilize his head and neck. Steve, you keep the crowd back and have them move their cars out of the road so the ambulance can get in," Chase instructed. He then showed Tyler how to hold Darren's head in alignment to prevent any further injury to his neck and spine. Chase began a head to toe assessment and kept an eye on Darren's breathing. He heard sirens approaching. "Thank God!" he sighed. He wasn't sure if he was doing this right.

The first to arrive was a deputy. He checked on Amanda; she was still okay. He saw Chase helping Darren then went back to direct traffic away from the scene. The ambulance arrived about a minute later. Chase was relieved to see them. The paramedic and E.M.T. quickly took over and prepared Darren for the trip to the hospital. They bandaged his chest with the turn signal lever still in place. The paramedic placed extra bandaging around it to prevent movement. Chase knew not to remove it because it could cause more damage. The E.M.T. splinted Amanda's arm, bandaged her head, then helped her into the ambulance. The ambulance left for the emergency room with the two patients.

Chase thanked his friends for helping, then watched the wrecker driver pull the mangled car from the ditch. I couldn't believe Darren and Amanda survived that crash. We found out later that Amanda was wearing her seatbelt and had not been thrown out. That probably saved her life. Darren was not wearing his seatbelt. His chest hit the steering wheel before he was thrown out.

Chase was very quiet on the ride home. He questioned himself over and over about how he handled his first aid treatment. He also questioned himself if he had what it took to be an E.M.T. "Rocky, that was the scariest thing I've ever done. I didn't know if I was really helping Darren or making him worse."

All I could do was snuggle next to him for comfort. What did I know about first aid? I was just a dog.

The next day Chase and I went to Trinity Emergency Medical Service. We caught up with the paramedic that came to the accident. "How are Amanda and Darren?" Chase asked.

John Wright, the paramedic, said, "He was drunk. The amount of alcohol in his blood was two times the legal limit. He was very lucky. The turn signal level went in sideways and barely missed puncturing his lung. He had a small fracture in his neck but you kept it from becoming a full break by showing your friend how to stabilize it. And, other than some scrapes and bruises, he's going to be okay. You did a good job out there."

"Really? Thank you! How about Amanda, how's she doing?"

"She broke her arm and had a small cut from the broken glass; that's about all. It would have been a different story if she hadn't been wearing her seatbelt."

"Is Darren going to be in trouble for drinking and driving?" Chase asked.

"He sure is. The deputy has charged him with Driving Under the Influence of Alcohol and Speeding. He will lose his driver's license; the cost of traffic fines, court fees, and lawyer fees will be thousands of dollars. His insurance rates will sky rocket and they might cancel his policy."

"What about his football scholarship?"

"He had a scholarship? He can kiss that goodbye."

Chase was quiet on the drive home. I could tell he was in deep thought. He went straight to his room, plopped on the bed, and stared at the ceiling.

Chase was going through an emotional roller coaster. "Rocky, you know, I'm glad I did the right treatment and I'm glad they're okay. But I'm mad that Darren was so stupid. He could have killed both of them. He has all but ruined his life and could have ruined Amanda's. I'm not sure if I really want to be an E.M.T. There's just too much grief."

When Lt. Carter came home from work, Mrs. Carter suggested he check on Chase. "He's still pretty depressed about the accident."

He went to Chase's room and sat on the bed next to him. "How's it going?"

"Not good. How long have you been a police officer?"

"Fourteen years."

"How do you do it every day? I mean, how do you deal with all the drama and trauma? How do you know if what you're doing is the right thing? What happens if you make a mistake? How do you handle someone dying?"

"Chase, those are all good questions. Every police officer, fire fighter, and paramedic has asked themselves those same questions at one time or another. Working in any type of emergency service is challenging, both physically and mentally. You have to know in your heart this is the job you want. When you know that, then you start training, lots of training. And you keep training throughout your career. Through training and experience you know how to do the right thing. If you make a mistake, correct it immediately, and own up to it. No one is perfect but in this line of work every mistake can be disastrous. That's why training is so important. Every call you go to is an opportunity to help someone. You get to save lives or prevent a life from being ruined. That's where the satisfaction comes from. I've watched people die. That is never easy. But whatever the reason for their death, you have to remember that you didn't put them in that situation. That happened before you ever got to the scene. Everything you do is to make it better, even if it's comforting the friends and family of the victim."

"But how do I know if I have what it takes?"

"Well, you have to be physically fit to be able to lift patients, move equipment, and get in and out of various scenes. That you have. You exercise and eat right, sometimes."

They both laughed.

"You need a good personality and must be able to get along and work well with other people. You have that. You must be patient. That one might need some work. You must be willing to spend long hours training and be willing to keep training. Your school work shows you can do that. And, perhaps most important, you must genuinely care about people. When you showed so much concern about your friends in the accident, you showed that you cared. Never lose your compassion. Chase, you have all the traits to make a good E.M.T., but that decision must be yours and yours alone. I suggest you pray about it."

"I will, Dad. Thanks." Chase thought about all the things his Dad had said.

Chapter Seven

A Big Surprise!

Chase jumped out of bed early the next morning and greeted his parents, "Good morning! It's a great day!" He ruffled my fur with his hands and kissed me on the head. "Morning Rocky! How's my favorite pooch?"

Fine, thank you. I was sure glad to see him in a better mood.

"You're certainly chipper. What's up?" his mother asked.

"I've made my decision. I want to be an E.M.T. and I want to be a paramedic. The college is offering a summer course for E.M.T.-Basic. Can I go? I don't want to wait until fall to begin my training."

His parents looked at each other and smiled. "Sure you can," his father replied, "Go see what you need to enroll."

Chase did enroll and began his classes that were five days a week. The E.M.T. Basic course involved a lot more than the First Responder class. He learned more anatomy and physiology, how to recognize the signs and symptoms of different illnesses and injuries, more advanced ways to take care of victims before they get to the hospital, how to prevent the spread of germs, and everything that goes in an ambulance. He also learned how to drive an ambulance. He said they handled a lot differently than his pickup. It was like driving a building down the road. *Wow! That can't be easy!*

I didn't get to spend much time with Chase that summer. He was either in school, studying, or spending time at Trinity Emergency Service. The medical director who oversees the operations of the service gave Chase permission to ride along with the crews on the weekends. Chase told me I could not ride in the ambulance because dogs aren't sanitary. *Humph!* I clean myself several times a day! I spent most of my time napping or finding ways to aggravate the cats when they weren't finding ways to aggravate me.

The test to be a registered Emergency Medical Technician-Basic was a lot harder than the one to be a First Responder. The questions on the written test were tough. Plus he had to do "practicals". In this part of the test, E.M.T.'s pretended to be patients. Better them than me! The student had to determine what was wrong and how to treat them. They were graded by other E.M.T.'s and Paramedics. Chase was exhausted after the tests.

"Man, I'm glad that's over! Now I have to wait weeks to find out if I passed."

Chase checked the mail every day to see if his results had come in. About three weeks later he received a letter. Chase tore open the envelope as he ran into the house. A letter and a patch fell out. "I passed! I passed!" he exclaimed.

"How do you know you passed if you haven't read the letter?" his mother asked.

"Ben said if you pass, they send your first patch with the letter. See? Here's the patch." Chase proudly held up the red, white, and blue patch with the words "Registered Emergency Medical Technician" around the emergency medical symbol. He then read the letter just to be absolutely sure. Yes, he had indeed passed. "Wahoo! I'm official!"

"I'm really proud of you! Call your father and tell him the good news."

Chase called his Dad and gushed the good news. His father was equally proud of him. Chase grabbed his pickup keys and said, "C'mon Rocky, let's go tell Ben."

Chase and I headed to the ambulance barn. Ben was in his office filling out some paper work. "Hey Ben, guess what?"

"You better say you passed your test."

"I did! See? Here's my patch." Chase proudly showed him the proof.

"Congratulations! Want a job?"

"Really? A job here? Doing what?"

"You're an E.M.T. now. Do you want a job working on an ambulance?"

"Are you kidding? Of course I do! Wow! Are you serious? When do I start?"

Ben laughed, "Chill. Yes I'm serious. We have an opening and you have been approved by the owners and the medical director. But I have one stipulation. This job is only part time because I want you to continue your training and become a paramedic. Agreed?"

"Absolutely!" Chase replied.

Chase and I went back home. He was still beaming. I was really proud of him too. He worked really hard for this. Yep, that's my boy!

Lt. Carter was home from work and greeted Chase with, "Congratulations again. Your Mom and I have a surprise for you. Go look on your bed."

Chase found a fully loaded jump kit waiting on his bed. A jump kit is a large bag or case that E.M.T.'s use when they "jump" from the ambulance and run to a scene. It contains all the things they might immediately need such as: bags attached to a face mask for rescue breathing, gloves, bandages, scissors, tape, small flashlight, blood pressure cuff, and other items. It also had a stethoscope. That's the thing with the tubes that go in your ears and a round metal thing at the other end to listen to a patient's breathing and heart rate. Hey, even I was learning some of this!

"We were confident you would pass so we bought the bag and have slowly added the contents," his mother explained.

"This is awesome! Thank you! You have perfect timing because I'm going to need this. Ben had more good news for me..."

"We know about the job," his father interrupted, "Ben talked to us about it before he made you the offer. We were in complete agreement that you could handle a part time job and school."

I remembered the first time I saw Chase in action. It was right in front of our house. Across the street lived a little boy named Timmy. He was the bully of the neighborhood. He would chase kids that were smaller than him, throw rocks at dogs (one hit me on the head) and poke sticks at the cats. He never minded his mother. What a brat!

On this afternoon, I was taking one of several daily naps on Chase's bed. My head was propped on the window sill that looked out over the front yard and across the street. Something woke me and I glanced out the window. I could see Timmy filling balloons with water from the garden hose. After he filled each balloon, he tied the ends, and gently placed them in a backpack. When the backpack was full, he slung it over his shoulder, and climbed up a tree in his front yard. About half way up, he stopped and hung the backpack over a branch. He carefully removed one of the bulging balloons and looked up the street.

What was he up to? Being the curious dog that I am, I went outside to get a closer look. Oh, I forgot to tell you. The Carters put in a larger pet door - just for me! Cool, uh? Anyway, I went to the side of the back yard where I could watch. My curiosity soon turned to anger when I realized what he was about to do. Mrs. Fischer, an elderly lady from up the street, was taking her daily walk with Fluff Fluff, her small white poodle. Timmy came to full alert from his perch within the tree. He raised back his hand that held the water filled balloon. Mrs. Fischer and Fluff Fluff were now just a few feet from the tree.

Oh no you don't! I let a series of loud barks that shook my paws. Fluff Fluff jumped straight up and into Mrs. Fischer's arms. She took a step back to keep her balance. Timmy didn't do quite as well. I had interrupted his timing, but he decided to launch the balloon anyway. As he threw the wet water bomb he lost his balance. The balloon hit the ground and splattered just in front of its intended victims. At the same time, Timmy landed on the ground with a hard thud. He quickly sat up, clutched his arm, and began screaming.

Mrs. Fischer rushed over to help Timmy. Fluff Fluff continuously scolded him with, "Yap! Yap! Yap!"

Timmy's mother ran out of the house. "Oh, my poor darling! What happened?"

"That stupid little dog scared me and made me fall!" Timmy cried as he pointed at Fluff Fluff.

You lying little brat.

Mrs. Carter came outside to see what was causing all the commotion. She saw Timmy crying and clutching his arm. His arm had a new bend between his wrist and elbow. "I'll call an ambulance. Don't let him move his arm."

A few minutes later I heard a siren and watched the ambulance stop in front of the house. Chase and his partner, John Wright, got out. Chase had his new jump kit. John was a paramedic and he was training Chase so he let him handle the call. Chase kneeled down by Timmy and talked calmly. "Let's take a look. Hurt pretty badly?"

"Yes!" Timmy sobbed.

"Okay, I'm going to make it feel better". He carefully placed a splint along the injured arm then gently wrapped it with gauze bandages. "See? This will keep it from moving so it won't hurt so much."

Timmy's screaming reduced to a whimper. Chase and John placed him on the stretcher and loaded him into the back of the ambulance. His mother was allowed to ride in the front seat as they took him to the emergency room.

Way to go, Chase!

A few hours later I saw a taxi pull up, and then Timmy and his mother get out. Timmy's arm was in a cast. The accident slowed him down - but only for a while.

Chase continued school and working part time. He passed the next hurdle and became a registered Emergency Medical Technician - Intermediate. Next step - Paramedic!

Chase saved money he earned from his job and bought a two-way radio for his pickup. He could communicate with the Trinity E.M.S. base station and respond to calls if he was nearby. It was cool when he responded to a call while in the pickup because I could go with him. The other E.M.T.'s liked when I was there if they had injured children. I kept them entertained while their wounds were bandaged. For some reason, when I was around, they didn't seem so scared. Maybe my help didn't seem like much, but it was great to be involved with Chase and the other rescuers.

Another year passed and Chase was ready to graduate from college. He completed all his courses and even took classes on search and rescue. He was also ready to take the ultimate test. He really worried about this one; after all, this is what his career dreams were about. "I don't think I'm ready. I need more time to study," he moaned to Ben.

"Chase, I felt the same way when I was ready to take the paramedic test. I don't think anyone ever really feels ready. It's a tough test. It has to be. Paramedics have a tremendous responsibility. You are trained to do more than you have ever done before. You have to be good at what you do. Remember, I have always said that you only get one chance to do the job right. We don't get do-overs. Now, having said all that, I know you can do this. I've asked you every question I could think of and you know the answers. I have watched you on the streets. You know your job inside and out. And most important, you care about your patients. When you take that test, answer each question as if it was for a real patient. You'll do fine."

Chase appreciated the encouragement from Ben but he was still worried about the test. I knew Chase could pass the test, I just wished he had the same confidence.

Six weeks had passed since Chase took the test for paramedic. Six long weeks and Chase was about to go stir crazy. He checked the mail every day. Some days he waited at the mail box for the mail man.

Finally one day the letter came. Chase clutched it in his hands and ran in the house. He sat on his bed and stared at the envelope.

Open it! I couldn't wait.

Chase's parents came into his room. "Well?" his mom asked.

"I haven't opened it yet."

"What are you waiting for? Let's see what it says," his dad said.

Chase slowly tore the seal on the envelope and shook the contents out. The letter slid out but nothing else. "I didn't pass. There's no patch." Chase moaned and walked out of his room.

His mother picked up the letter, read it, and called, "Chase, you might want to look at this."

Chase came back and took the letter from her. It said he had passed his test but they were out of paramedic patches and would send one soon.

"Wahoo!" Chase yelled.

"Congratulations son, we're very proud of you. Let's go out to dinner to celebrate!" his father invited.

Of course you know dogs aren't allowed in restaurants, so I had to wait at home. Chase did bring back a steak bone for me. *Yum!*

Ben called Chase that same evening and sounded unusually serious. "I need you to come in. We have to talk about something."

"What's going on?" Chase asked.

"We'll talk about it when you get here."

"Okay, I'll be there shortly." Chase hung up the phone and wondered what was wrong. He told his parents he was going to the ambulance barn and called for me to come with him. His parents said they were going to the store and would see us when they got back. All the way in, Chase tried to imagine what Ben wanted. Was he going to be fired? Were they closing the E.M.S. Service? Was he being sued?

When we arrived, we went straight to Ben's office. Ben stood up and said, "Follow me."

"What's going on?" Chased asked again.

"You'll see." Ben said as he hid a smile.

When they reached the ambulance barn at the back of the building Ben turned on the lights. The entire crew was standing in front of the row of ambulances. They were holding a large handmade banner that read, "Congratulations Ben and Chase!" The walls and ceiling of the barns had been decorated with streamers. Chase's parents were holding a cake that also said congratulations to the two. Chase knew why he was being con-gratulated but not Ben. He looked at Ben.

"Let me explain. Part of this celebration is for you becoming a paramedic, but there is more - a lot more. I had some good news today also. I found out I've been accepted into medical school. That's been a dream of mine."

"That's great! Congratulations!" said Chase.

"Wait, there's more," Ben continued. "Now that I'm leaving, they'll need someone to be the E.M.S. supervisor and director of search and rescue operations. That someone is you."

"Me?" Chase asked in disbelief. "Why me?"

"You're the logical choice. You've had the most training in search and rescue. You also have taken college courses in E.M.S. management. You have more than proven you are capable of handling just about any situation that gets thrown at you. And the crews voted for you," Ben explained.

Everyone began clapping and cheering for Chase and Ben. Chase was still trying to let it all soak in. Could this day get any better?

"Oh, one last thing. Here." Ben tossed a set of keys to Chase. They were the keys to Ben's monster size rescue truck.

Chase felt like he was living a dream.

After the party, Chase and I climbed into the rescue truck. I was allowed to ride along because it only carried equipment, no patients. Chase turned the ignition and listened to the rumble of the powerful engine. We pulled out of the ambulance barn and headed for home.

"Can you believe all this? My ultimate dream has come true! Rocky, we finally made it!"

Yes, we, uh, you did. I was so proud of him.

Neither of us knew he would be initiated into his new job so quickly.

Chapter Eight

Collapsed Building - Workers Trapped!

We were about a mile from home when the dispatcher called Chase over the radio, "Adam One, Code 3. 4501 East Lamont. Building collapsed. Workers trapped."

Chase laughed, "They're just messing with us." Chase flipped on the scanner and heard the police and fire departments being dispatched to the same location. Chase took a deep breath and acknowledged the dispatcher with "10-4". He activated the red lights and siren on the big rig and made a u-turn. "Rocky, this is for real. Are we ready?"

You bet we are! At least I know you are. I thought I could hear my heart pounding over the siren.

We arrived about two minutes later and saw what had been an old brick and concrete, two story office building. Most of the second floor had collapsed into the first floor. Smoke and dust were still rising from the rubble. A police officer had already arrived at the scene and was talking to two men wearing hard hats. They were excitedly trying to explain what happened as we ran up. One said he was the foreman and that his crew had been hired to tear down the old building so a new one could be built in its place. The owner had offered large bonuses if they could complete the job within a week. The workers agreed to work late every night to meet the deadline. Apparently they had been in too much of a hurry and did not use all the safety precautions. The foreman said five of the workers were still trapped inside.

Chase would have to call on all his training and experience for this rescue. As other emergency workers arrived they gathered around their new leader for instructions. Chase immediately began briefing, organizing, and directing the rescue operation.

The first consideration was the safety of the rescuers and the trapped workers. He asked the foreman if the building had any electrical or natural gas lines running to it. The foreman said the utilities had been turned off before they began work. Chase instructed the foreman to get the floor plans of the building and show him where the trapped workers were last seen. He also wanted a list of any hazardous materials that might be in the building. The collapse could have caused containers of hazardous materials to rupture and leak. Flood lights powered by generators were erected on top of the fire trucks to illuminate the scene.

Chase's dad arrived at the scene. He said the police officers were setting up a road block around the area to keep out curiosity seekers. Bystanders often want to get involved in the action, and some hope they will have an opportunity to be a hero. Although most have good intentions, they don't have the proper training. Some have become victims themselves because they tried to help and ended up getting hurt. Some spectators are so curious that they actually get in the way of the rescue operations and must be told to leave. Time is very critical in these situations and the rescuers must spend every minute on the rescue - not crowd control.

The rescuers assigned to the scene began slowly and carefully removing surface debris. Moving too quickly or suddenly could cause further collapse of the weakened building. In a situation like this, the rescuers assume that all the victims are alive until proven otherwise.

The rescue operation had barely started when one of the fire fighters shouted, "I found one!" Two more fire fighters and two E.M.T.'s rushed over to help. The other rescuers fought the urge to join the recovery. They are all trained to save lives and, when a rescuer actually sees a victim, it's hard for the others to stay in their assigned areas. They may dig for hours and not find anyone, but they know their responsibility and continue to work.

The first victim had been walking toward one of the building's exits when the collapse occurred. He was in a narrow stairway and the heavier debris had fallen away from him. He was conscious and his only injuries seemed to be a sprained ankle some scrapes, and a few bruises. An ambulance crew took him to the emergency room to be checked out more thoroughly.

The search continued for the other four victims. Piece by piece, bricks and other debris were removed from the rubble. Jack hammers and air chisels had to be used to break up the heavier pieces and rebar. Occasionally, Chase would call for a "stop". All equipment was turned off and no one whispered a word. In the still of the night, the only sounds would be the rescuers' own hearts pounding with anticipation. They were listening for sounds of life beneath their feet, a cry for help, a moan, or slight movement. They listened for any sound that would renew their hopes that the other four workers were alive.

Nothing.

The search and rescue operation continued into the night. After 4 hours, there was still no sign of the remaining victims. I had been intently watching the workers and feeling totally useless.

"Rocky." Chase said my name and I about jumped out of my fur. "We sure could use your help right now."

Do what?

He continued, "I bet you could smell where those victims are. Will you try?"

You want me to help? Wow! I was glad I didn't have a cold or stuffy nose. Okay, nose, we've got a job to do. And a dog's gotta do what a dog's gotta do!

Chase called for another "stop". All the workers sat their tools down. Silence fell over the scene as all eyes were on me. *Gee, no pressure here...*

Chase led me across the rubble. We slowly canvassed the area and my nose remained in the full alert mode. I have never wanted to do something correctly as much as I did this. We covered about half of the area and I found nothing.

Nose, please don't fail me. Please don't fail Chase. And, most of all, please don't fail those trapped workers.

I scanned my nose over an area and detected a different odor. I stopped and sniffed again. Not wanting to make a fool of myself, I stuck my nose deep into the debris and took in a long sniff.

Achoo! Achoo!

My nose had sucked up some of the dust. Through the dust I detected the distinct smell of humans! The smell was fairly strong which indicated the humans were in great fear and that meant they were still alive. I immediately began barking, dancing around, and pawing at the area. In my excitement, I began trying to dig out the victim by myself. Paws are not made to move bricks and concrete!

"Good work, Rocky!" Chase exclaimed as he pulled me out of the rescuers' way.

About two feet down, they found three of the construction workers. One was unconscious but breathing, the other two were awake and in a lot of pain. The rescuers were able to free them after about thirty minutes of digging. These three were also transported to the emergency room.

We were still missing one worker.

I continued my smell search but could not detect anything or anyone. I poked my nose in every hole and re-sniffed every inch. Still nothing. I was getting frustrated and so were the rescuers. Six hours had passed since the collapse of the building. Chase sighed, "I hope his time hasn't run out." He was worried that the last trapped worker might have run out of air or succumbed to serious injuries. The rescuers were tired and my nose was sore. No one complained; they just kept digging.

Where was the fifth victim?

I passed over an area I had been over before. This time something made me stop in my tracks. It was a small, faint smell. Was it human? I couldn't tell so I kept sniffing. I had the feeling that the trapped worker was below me but the smell was so faint and something else was interfering with the scent. I looked at Chase and whimpered. I didn't want to get anyone's hopes up, but I wanted to know for sure.

Chase said a silent prayer and called the other rescuers to our spot. The night had been long and the rescuers were near exhaustion. The hope that the last victim had been found and the slim chance he was still alive brought renewed energy. Everyone began digging and tossing bricks and other debris until someone shouted, "I see him!" A hand and arm was sticking through the rubble.

A strong odor of gasoline surrounded the victim. The workers had been using gasoline powered equipment and some of the liquid must have spilled in this area. No wonder I had trouble smelling!

Chase felt the wrist and detected a faint pulse. "He's alive," Chase reported, then in almost a whisper, "but barely."

Those words had just left Chase's mouth when we felt a rumble beneath us.

"Run!" the construction foreman yelled.

All the rescuers barely cleared the area before the rest of the second floor crashed to the first floor. The area that we had just been standing on was covered with more bricks and concrete.

All the rescuers stared wide-eyed at this newest horrible event. Chase's head dropped and I saw a tear fall from his eye. "The last victim, the last victim..." Chase was too upset to finish the sentence. The other rescuers hung their heads in silence. Everyone knew the chances of the last construction worker surviving the second collapse were almost zero.

Chase and I walked back to the area where, just a few moments earlier, a living person lied buried alive and clinging to life. Chase ran his hand over the rubble. I could see the hurt in his eyes. It wasn't the kind of hurt like when your stump your paw. This was much deeper. I wanted to comfort him but I didn't know how.

Lt. Carter walked up and put his arm around his son. "Chase, you did a good job. The hospital said the four workers are going to be fine. You did everything you could for the last one."

I felt so sorry for Chase, the other rescuers, and the last victim. Everyone was so sad, so tired, so…

What was that? I wasn't sure if I smelled something, or if I heard something, or if I just sensed something. Something was under my paws and that something was human. I barked and pawed the ground.

Chase patted my head and said, "I know Rocky. That's where the last victim is, somewhere under all these bricks. Well, let's finish up and dig out the body."

I felt in my heart that the victim was still alive but I couldn't make Chase understand. He was too caught up in his grief and fatigue.

He released most of the rescuers. The rest stayed to help Chase with the last dig. Another hour passed before they had dug to the last spot he was seen before the second collapse. I kept whimpering and pawing the area. The feeling that he was still alive was becoming more intense. Chase pulled me out of the way and kept digging. He tossed some bricks out of the way and saw an incredible sight. When the rest of the building collapsed, a large steel beam had fallen across the victim. It would have landed directly on him but each end was balanced on a pile of bricks and debris. Not only did the beam save him from being crushed, it formed an air pocket that allowed him to breath.

He was alive!

Chase and two fire fighters gently pulled him from the rubble. There was no time for cheers, his injuries were critical. The last construction worker was rushed to the hospital where he underwent emergency surgery. It would take a long time for him to get well but he did recover.

Before we left for the hospital, Chase put his arm around me and said, "I owe you an apology. You knew where the last construction worker was and you knew he was alive. You tried to let me know but I was too caught up in my own grief. From now on I'll trust when you are trying to tell me something. I'm so proud of you!"

Gee, thanks! No need for an apology. That was a first for both of us.

The day after the rescue, the owner of the construction company presented each rescuer a certificate of appreciation. He gave me a big raw hide bone wrapped with a blue bow. *Thanks!* That wasn't my only reward of the day. The E.M.T's bought me a new red collar that had my rabies tag plus another tag. In the middle of that tag was the "Star of Life" emblem. That's the blue emblem you see on ambulances. It is the symbol for emergency medical services. Around the emblem was engraved "Rocky Rescue". I was so proud to have been part of the team that saved five lives that day. I wished I could do more.

Chapter Nine

K-9 SAR School

A few days after the rescue of the trapped construction workers, we were eating at the local drive-in with some of the other crews. Chase was having his usual grilled chicken salad with low fat dressing. He had become very health conscious which really annoyed me. I mean, all the exercising and weight lifting was okay. And I enjoyed when we'd go jogging, but this health food craze was for the birds. Give me a double cheeseburger any day! Like the one was I chomping down on.... *"Ptew! Who put the pickle in there?"*

Mr. Stafford, the owner of Trinity Emergency Medical Service, drove up. "Hi guys! How is everybody? Rocky, always good to see you, in fact you're why I'm here."

Who, me?

"Hey, Mr. Stafford! What's up?" Steve asked.

"I'm here to make a proposal to Chase and Rocky. Chase, I heard good reports on how you orchestrated the rescue. Everyone did a great job and certainly lived up to their training. Rocky did a fantastic job without any training. I think he should have more."

More what?

"You mean S.A.R. training?" Chase asked.

"I think you and Rocky would make a great search and rescue team. If you're interested, I'd like to send both of you to the school."

"Wow! That's awesome!" Chase explained.

It sounds good, but I don't know how to read. Maybe Chase could read to me. How could I take the tests? I don't have thumbs to hold a pencil. I wondered how the other dogs made it through the school. Did they stay up late studying? Has any dog ever skipped school? What if I'm really stupid and flunk? What if...

"We'll do it!" Chase said as he shook Mr. Stafford's hand to seal the deal.

Oh boy, I hope I don't embarrass anyone.

"Rocky, this is going to be great. We'll have so much fun and, best of all, you'll be an official Search and Rescue dog!"

Wow! I'll be official. What does official mean?

"We'll have to get you in shape," Chase continued.

What do you mean "get in shape"? I am in shape. I'm in the shape of a dog.

"Of course this means you have to eat healthier. No more cheeseburgers."

Groan. I'm willing to make some sacrifices for the cause, but isn't this going a bit too far?

"Okay, I see that look you're giving me. How about just one a week?"

I can live with that.

We watched a police car drive up. "K-9" was painted in white letters on the side of the unit. "Caution: Police dog" was stenciled on the dark tinted rear windows. A female officer stepped out. It was Amanda Skyler.

"Hi Chase!" She said as she sat down next to us.

"Hello, Amanda." My Dad said you joined the police department. How long have you been with the K-9 division?"

"About a year. I have a Belgian Malinois. She looks a little like a German Sheppard and her name is Sasha. Right now she's just trained in narcotic detection but the Chief is going to send us to S.A.R. training next month. I'm really looking forward to it. So, how have you been? I haven't seen you since the accident. I kept telling myself I needed to call and thank you for helping out there, but I was too embarrassed. I was so stupid to go with Darren when I knew he had been drinking."

"Don't worry about that. We were young and dumb. I'm glad everything turned out so well for you. Did you say you're going to Search and Rescue training? Rocky and I are going, too."

"Hey, that's great! Why don't you come to the police department's training field? We have an agility course set up like they will use in the school. It will be good practice for your dog. His name is Rocky?"

"Rocky Rescue," Chase replied. "Sounds great."

"Sasha and I will be out there tomorrow morning. See you then!"

Amanda left and I didn't have a chance to meet Sasha. I couldn't wait. I heard Belgian Malinois dogs were really good looking.

The next morning Chase and I were up early. Chase was still reeling in excitement about the S.A.R. school and that Amanda was also going.

"Life is good, Rocky!" Chase beamed as he spent extra time styling his hair.

I totally agreed while giving my coat an extra grooming.

We went to the Bethany Police Department's training field and waited for Amanda. She arrived a few minutes later.

"Hi guys!" She greeted us as she opened the back door of the police car.

The most beautiful dog I have ever seen stepped from the back. She shook her shiny gold fur and then looked at me. Her face and ear tips were black. Her eyes were a rich brown. Her body was trim and well muscled. I was in love.

"C'mon. I'll take Sasha through the course so you can see what to do."

Chase and I watched intently. Amanda's long ponytail bounced as she ran the course with her dog. Sasha took each obstacle with such grace it was almost like she was performing a choreographed dance. I think we should have been watching what they did instead of just them. When they finished, Amanda asked Chase if we were ready to try it.

"Uh, oh, uh," Chase had become tongue tied. Amanda was so pretty and Chase seemed to still have a crush on her.

"Don't be nervous, it's really fun," Amanda encouraged as she led us to the beginning of the course.

I was eager to impress Sasha with skills I hadn't learned yet. Bad mistake. The first obstacle was two rows of olds car tires that I was suppose to run through. My front legs weren't communicating with my back legs. I tripped several times before finally landing muzzle down in the grass. The next one looked easier. It was a wood platform with planks on each side to run up. That was easy. Next was a metal drainage pipe used to simulate a tunnel - that was also easy. Then there was another drainage pipe that was longer and curved into an "S" shape. That was a little spooky at first because it was really dark. I had to climb up and over a pile of rocks and bricks - nothing to it.

And then there was the ladder. Ladders are not made for paws. Dogs are not made for ladders. I was supposed to climb about a gazillion rungs to the roof of a storage shed. I sat at the bottom and looked up. The sun was shining so brightly in my eyes that I couldn't see the top. I bet heaven was at the top. Chase was encouraging me and saying he knew I could do it. Okay, a search and rescue dog has to do what a search and rescue dog has to do. One paw at a time I pulled my furry body upward. About half way up, my legs began to ache. I wished I could use my tail as a fifth leg. Then a really dumb idea struck me. Chase and Amanda were busy talking and Sasha was watching a boy on a bicycle. I decided to cheat. I thought if I could take two rungs at a time I could get this over quicker. I skipped the next rung and wrapped my paw around the second one. As I pulled myself up, my back right leg tried to find a rung. Where did it go? My left leg couldn't find it either. My front paw lost its gripped and I slid all the way back down to the bottom. I landed with a thud on my tail end. Chase and Amanda immediately ran over to see if I was all right. The only thing hurting was my pride. Sasha came up and licked my head. I bet she was thinking I was a poor excuse for a S.A.R. dog. After shaking off the humiliation I looked at that ladder with a new determination. A dog's gotta do what a dog's gotta do. I jumped on the ladder and slowly made my way to the top. When I reached the roof Chase and Amanda were cheering. Sasha gave me a bark of congratulations. I did it!

Then there was the round log suspended above the ground that I had to walk across. That was a little tricky because I had to keep my balance so I wouldn't fall off. I had to low crawl under a wood platform that wasn't tall enough for me to stand up.

The last obstacle took the longest. Hundreds of hay bales were stacked and arranged into a maze. Chase led me to the opening and told me to wait. He ran to the other side and out of my sight. The walls of this hay maze were high enough that I could not see over them. I heard Chase yell, "Rocky, come!" I took off through the maze in search of my partner. Every few turns I ran into a dead end and had to find my way back out. I was getting frustrated and called out to Chase with a bark. He called my name again. I ran this way and that way, dead end after dead end. Finally! I found the other end and Chase. He hugged me and said I did a good job. Good job? I didn't think I was ever going to get out of there. I was imagining the fire department coming to my rescue. Overall I felt I did a lousy job. I was slow and clumsy. I sure couldn't have impressed Sasha.

Amanda told Chase, "Rocky did great for his first time. He never gave up. That's a good indication he'll do well in the school."

We went back to the training field several times a week before my school started. I worked extra hard to become proficient on all the obstacles and to make Chase proud. If Chase is happy, I'm happy.

The Search and Rescue Dog School was about an hour away in the rolling mountains in the northern part of the state. The setting was both spectacular in beauty and variety of terrain.

Almost every type of search scenario could be found. Dense forests with thick and sparse underbrush opened to valleys of short grass and crystal clear streams. The mountains offered rocky climbs and dark caves. In the winter, the mountains became covered with snow which made for great avalanche training. Chase and I were eager to begin school.

The first day of school was orientation. We met twenty other teams. I have never seen so many dogs in my life. There were German Sheppards, Labradors, Belgian Malanois's like Sasha, and I even met a few dogs that looked like me. I wondered if I was related to any of the other Strays. After the meet and greet, we gathered in a large auditorium to meet the instructors. They all had years of experience in K-9 search and rescue. They explained what we would learn and how we would be graded.

They also explained that there are two types of training for search and rescue dogs. One is tracking and the other is air-scenting. We would be learning air- scenting. We would have to prove that we were eager to learn, able to follow a scent, always listened to our handler (I prefer to think of Chase as my partner), and be willing to work long hours in all types of weather. This was going to be so much fun. I couldn't wait!

After listening to the orientation, the instructors collected the veterinary forms. We had to show that we were in good health and had all our vaccinations. We were then assigned to a cabin. How cool is that? We get to stay in a real log cabin! The female handlers and their dogs had their own cabin. The male handlers were divided between two cabins because there were more of us. The handlers spent the rest of the afternoon getting to know each other and talking about where they were from and what kind of work they did. There were police officers, E.M.T.'s, paramedics, and two from the U.S. Army. I had a great time playing with the other dogs. A white German Sheppard named Riley became my new best friend. We took a tour of the grounds and made a practice run together through the agility course just for fun. When it was time for supper, we all gathered back in the auditorium. Rows of tables were set up for the handlers. The dogs had their suppers brought from home. The last thing the instructors wanted was a dog with an upset tummy from eating food they weren't accustomed to. Riley and his E.M.T. partner Daniel sat to our right. Sasha and Amanda sat to our left. Life is sweet!

About half way through the meal, a big bully of a mixed breed named Kong had quickly finished his supper and started looking around for more. He tried to muzzle his way into Thor's bowl. Thor was an easy going black Labrador. That is, easy going until someone tries to steal his food. A fight ensued and the handlers quickly scrambled to separate them. One of the cardinal rules of the school and future work of S.A.R. dogs is that they must get along with the other dogs and handlers. The instructors told them this was their first warning. One more and they would be kicked out of the school.

The next morning we were given an early wake up call. After breakfast we assembled in the agility field. One at a time, each handler took his (or her) dog through the course. Everyone did really great. The agility course was the first thing we did every morning of the school. I like it because it helped me limber up for the training exercises.

After each run through the agility course, we went to the auditorium for class room instruction. The first class was all about air scent. We learned that humans constantly loose tiny, tiny, too tiny to see, skin cells called rafts. These rafts hold the smell that is unique to that human. As these rafts slough off they float away from the person on drafts of air. Some linger in the air, some fall on the ground or surrounding vegetation, some cling to other surfaces such as clothing or furniture, and others are whisked around by the wind. They drift downwind from the human in the shape of a cone. The farther away from the person, the wider the cone becomes and the weaker the smell. Dogs can detect smells a gazillion times better than a human. We are able to smell these rafts and follow them to the human. Pretty cool, eh?

We learned that cool air sinks so the smells will be closer to the ground in cold weather. Warm air rises so the scent will be higher up. Moist air holds the smell better than dry air. Moist dog noses detect smell better than dry noses. Rafts that settle on water can be carried down- stream where they eventually float to the top and can be carried again by the wind. I didn't know there were so many different things a smell could do. My nose was certainly going to get a work out. I can't wait to try it!

After indoor class we went back outside to another large field. The first training exercise was pretty simple. I had to have my lead on (still don't know why). Daniel held me by the lead while Chase walked away. He kept saying, "Bye Rocky! I'm leaving! Here I go!" I see that. *Wait! I want to go with you but Daniel won't let me. Hackity! I want to go!* Chase walked about a hundred feet or so then ducked behind a tree. At the same time, Daniel released my lead and said, "Rocky, find!" He didn't have to tell me twice. I made a bee line to where Chase was hiding. Chase grabbed me in a hug and said, "Good boy! That was great!" Daniel also came up, patted me on the head, and said I did greatl.

We took turns with Riley and Daniel a few more times before the instructors changed the plan. This time, Daniel took me behind a wall so I couldn't see where Chase went. Very tricky! After Chase hid, the instructor signaled for Daniel to let me go. Daniel released my lead and said, "Rocky, find!" Oh boy! Here I go! Okay where did Chase go? I smelled him but I didn't see him. *Oh, duh!* That's the whole idea! I stuck my nose in the air and followed Chase's scent to where he was hiding behind another tree. Again he hugged me and said, "Good boy!" Daniel and the instructor came over and gave me a big hug. Chase and I wrestled around on the ground in celebration. I love school!

We watched the other teams go through their exercises. Most of them did really well. One blond Labrador (this is not a blond joke) was having a bit of a problem concentrating. The first time she was released and told to "Find" she headed toward her handler. She was saying, "Here I come! I'll find you! I'm almost there. Here I... Ooh! A rabbit!" And off she went after the furry little critter. The instructor had her try again. This time she found her handler but only after stopping to smell and eat a daisy. She didn't make it through the class because she couldn't concentrate. We hated to see her go. She was really nice and was always encouraging the other dogs to do their best.

Another dog that didn't make it to the end was Kong. He was too busy being a bully. Twice he got away from his handler and jumped on another dog that was having problems with an exercise. The final straw was when he bit an instructor on the back side when he bent over to pick up dropped cell phone.

One team was kicked out because of the handler. He had a Belgian Malinois that was really trying hard. Every time his dog made the slightest mistake he would yell at him and call him "Stupid" or "Worthless". He never praised him when he did an exercise correctly. He even whipped the dog with the leather lead. Not only were they dismissed from the school, but the instructors sent a letter to his department stating he should not be a dog handler. Chase found out later that his dog was given to another handler who treated him like royalty. Thank goodness!

The next classes became increasingly complex. I went from finding Chase to searching for Daniel. We were given different places to search and had to go through different types of terrain to find the "victim". Sometimes the instructors would be the ones to hide so we would have different scents to follow. The toughest challenge was when an instructor made numerous turns through the woods, walked across a stream, then circled back to the starting point. It took me a while to figure it out but I eventually found him. Chase and the instructor gave me big hugs and lots of praise. I'm not sure who was having the most fun, me or Chase!

We were given a new challenge that involved finding several "victims". Chase and I started at the outer edge of the forest when he gave me the command, "Rocky, find!" I put my nose in the air and immediately found a scent. It didn't take long before I found the instructor hiding behind a bush. "Great job! Rocky, find!" Chase said.

Find? I just found him. *Don't you see him?*

"We've got more to find. Rocky, go find!"

Oh, now I get it! Okay nose; let's see who else is out here.

I followed the scents and found four more people hiding in different places. This was like solving a giant puzzle and each success was followed by lots of praise. I hoped the other teams were having as much fun.

The next day was class room for our human partners. They learned how to read maps and how to use a compass and G.P.S. Riley, Sasha, and I played with the other dogs in the agility field. When that became boring, we headed to the pond. This was built especially for the school. It was only about four feet deep in the middle. It was deep enough that we had to dog paddle to get around but shallow enough for the instructor and our handler to help us learn how to detect scents on the water. They also had a small boat anchored just off the shore. We used that for a diving board. After class our partners came outside and watched us playing in the water. Of course, we all had to do what dogs do, we ran to the humans and shook our wet coats all over them. Everyone was laughing and soaking wet. We played group tag until called for supper.

The next day was all about becoming familiar with different types of transportation. Search and rescue teams sometimes have to go into areas not accessible by car. We sat on the back of a snow mobile and took a short ride on a ski lift. That was really cool, I could see for miles from up there. We climbed around in a big boat and tried on life jackets.

We heard a "thup, thup thup" in the distance that was slowly getting louder. A helicopter was flying into the field. That was awesome! After it landed, we took turns getting in and out. We practiced getting in during a "hot load". That means boarding while the engine is running and the blades are rotating. The humans had to remember to duck to avoid the blades. We took rides around the mountains. Helicopters are noisy! I wanted to ask one of the crew if I could borrow their head phones but it was too loud for them to hear me. My first ride was scary. This big metal bird was shaking and my tummy was not happy. The pilot told us to look out the open door. Wait, open door? *Hey! Who forgot to close the door in this thing!* We weren't the only team to look a little green after the first flight. It took a few more practice trips to get use to flying. I can't say it ever became fun, definitely interesting, but never really fun.

Another thing we learned was about all the equipment we would need. Some of the items for the handler were: backpack, water bottles, helmet, leather gloves, climbing harness, first aid kit, maps, compass, G.P.S., and radio. The dog's list included: collar, identification tag, a 6 foot and 30 foot lead, toys (most important), travel bowls for food and water (second most important), harness, booties... *Booties?* What self respecting dog would wear booties? When the instructors handed out the booties they gave me a pink pair. Pink rubber doggie booties! *You have got to be kidding!* Sasha was given a blue pair which I gladly traded. The instructors said we would find out tomorrow why we might sometimes need them.

The next morning the handlers struggled with putting on our new paw apparel. *Who designed these things?* Several of us tried shaking them off. That didn't work. We tried walking in them. That was awkward. Some of the dogs were taking giant steps while others kept walking backwards as if trying to walk away from these unnatural contraptions. Our handlers laughed as we attempted to walk to the next training exercise. This was a small building that had been constructed then partially bulldozed to simulate a collapsed building. *Been there - done that!* This one was a bit different than the one Chase and I had been in with the trapped construction workers. In addition to chunks of bricks and concrete, there were broken boards with nails sticking out and shattered glass. Now I see why we have booties. I agreed they were necessary equipment but was glad to get them off after the exercise.

Our partners were taught first aid for dogs and what to carry in their K-9 first aid kit. I warned Riley and Sasha about what happened to me for pretending to be a patient. They rolled on the ground laughing. It wasn't funny! I told them how I fell on the sleeping cat and had a collision with a flower vase. They laughed harder. At first I was mad but the more I thought about it, the more I realized it really was funny. I hobbled around on 3 legs and acted like I was splinted and bandaged. The three of us rolled on the ground laughing until are tummies hurt.

We had so much more to learn and Chase and I loved every minute of it. I couldn't believe I was training for a job that gave me an opportunity to save lives and work side by side with Chase. This didn't seem like a job, it was fun! Let me skip ahead here. After the basic school we returned to our jobs at Trinity Emergency Medical Service. Once a month we went back to the S.A.R. school for more training. It took about 18 months to complete the school; then Chase and I became certified in Search and Rescue. The training didn't end there. Once a month we met with Amanda, Sasha, Daniel, and Riley at different locations to practice and train. Once a year we all went back to our Search and Rescue School for refresher training and updates. When you're in the business of saving lives, you can never get enough training and you never stop learning.

Back at work, we settled into our routine. Of course, nothing stays "routine" long in the E.M.S. business.

Chapter Ten

Strangely Familiar

Now that Chase and I were certified in search and rescue, we were anxious for our first mission. That didn't come until about a month after the school. We still had the job of making emergency calls with the other E.M.T.'s and Paramedics. I rode with Chase in our monster Search and Rescue truck to the scenes. It was always interesting to watch rescuers at work. At every call I felt I learned something new. I also learned that not every call is a life or death situation.

We were dispatched to a house just a few blocks from the ambulance barn. The dispatcher told us a lady had her head stuck in a fish bowl. Did I hear that right? When we arrived a man met us on the front porch. He said, "My crazy wife! I can't believe she could be so stupid! I offered to use my hammer to get the blasted bowl off but she insisted on calling an ambulance. See what you can do."

I sat on the porch and watched through the door. There she sat at the dining room table with a round fish bowl firmly wedged upside down on her head. She was using both hands to push and pull but it wouldn't budge. Chase asked her husband if they had any cooking grease or oil.

What's he going to do - cook her head out of there?

The husband went to the kitchen and came back with a can of cooking grease. Chase put rubber gloves on and squished his hands into the gooey white grease. He then rubbed his slippery gloved hands around the lady's neck. He reached inside the bowl as far as possible with his fingers and smeared more of the grease around her face, ears, and head. He removed the gloves and gave a couple of tugs on the glass bowl. *Floop!* The bowl slid off. Chase let her catch her breath before asking the obvious question.

"Why? Why did I do this? I'll tell you why," she replied while wiping globs of grease from her face. "My husband spends hours looking at his stupid fish. I wanted to know what it looked like to them with his big mug against their bowl."

"Yes," her husband answered back. "And you dumped my expensive fish into a salad bowl! You've done some dumb stunts before but this one takes the cake."

The two continued to argue but Chase interrupted, "Are you two going to be okay?"

The couple angrily looked at each other then smiled. "Sure we are. We fuss all the time. It never really means anything;

we're just blowing off steam." She said as she rested her greasy head on her husband's shoulder. He placed his arm around her and they laughed about the whole incident.

I bet living with them would never be dull!

Our first official search and rescue mission came on a late afternoon. Chase and I were off duty and driving around in the country looking at houses for sale. Chase had been saving money for a long time and finally had enough for a down payment. "Beep! Beep! Beep!" Chase's pager alerted him that a message was coming in. It read, "Wichita National Park - Campsite 7-B, lost 5 year old." Chase called dispatch and advised we would pick up the rescue truck, then would head that way.

"Well, Rocky, here comes our first mission. Actually it will be your mission since you'll be doing all the work. Is your nose ready?" Chase asked.

You betcha'! I couldn't wait to try out my new skills. Even though Chase was driving Code 3 with lights and siren, I wished we could go faster. Chase was a very careful driver. He always told new E.M.T.'s in training that you can't help a victim if you crash and can't get to them.

When we arrived at Campsite 7-B, we saw Deputy Sawyer talking to the very anxious parents. The family had enjoyed a picnic and was packing to return home. Their seven year old son, Matthew, was helping pack. Their five year old daughter, Lisa, was chasing butterflies. When the mother placed the last items in the car, she turned around and could not see Lisa. They searched for their daughter for an hour then decided they would need help.

This camp site was set in a clearing and surrounded by dense forest. About 300 feet beyond the forest was the Trinity River. This was a large river that snaked through the park, forked at the south end, and separated the three counties. It had fast water and was often used for white water rafting. Deputy Sawyer asked if they had tried calling her name. The father, looking near panic stricken, said, "It wouldn't do any good. She's deaf. "

This news made the situation even more urgent. Chase said we had better get started and placed my vest on me. It was bright red with the words "Search and Rescue" written on both sides in white letters. Yellow reflective tape bordered the top and sides. When the vest went on I knew it was time to go to work. The mother showed us the last place she saw Lisa. She had been walking along a small stream near the campsite as she tried to catch butterflies in a paper cup.

Chase gave the command I had been waiting for, "Rocky, find!"

I held my nose in the air and a flood of different scents surrounded me. I had to quickly sort them. Okay, there's Chase's scent, there's the father's scent, there's Deputy Sawyer's scent, there's the mother's scent, there's the son's scent, and there's another scent. It was similar to the family's scents but uniquely different. That must belong to Lisa.

I followed the scent into the woods. Children are different than adults, especially the really young ones. At first, they wander around looking at things of interest such as butterflies, rocks, and flowers. When they realize they are lost, fear sets in. Most have no experience in finding their way back so they usually keep wandering deeper into the remote area. This seemed to be true with Lisa. I followed her zigzag scent from groups of blooming wild flowers, to a pile of rocks in the stream, and to bush covered with yellow butterflies. Her scent continued deeper into the forest.

Chase and Deputy Sawyer followed behind. The rest of the family was asked to stay at the camp site in case Lisa returned and so their scent would not interfere with hers.

We only had about another hour of daylight. This wasn't a problem for me because dog's have great night vision. It could be a problem for Lisa because she would not be able to see where she was going. She could fall into a hole, trip over a fallen tree limb, be bitten by an unseen snake, or tumble into the river.

Her scent remained strong and fortunately the density of the trees prevented the wind from blowing the scent around. I found her pink hair ribbon that had caught on a low tree branch. It wasn't long before we could hear the roar of the Trinity River. Chase said a prayer that she hadn't made it that far. She had. Her scent led me to the edge of the bank. Twenty feet below, the water rushed and crashed against large boulders in its path. Chase and I knew a fall would probably not be survivable. I did a slow circle and tried to pinpoint where her scent went. I breathed a sigh of relief as I found it moving away from the river. Her scent became stronger and I knew she was close. I started running with Chase and Deputy Sawyer trying to keep up. I jumped over a large fallen tree and almost did a back flip before landing on the other side. In mid air, I saw a small figure huddled against the trunk. I immediately started barking with excitement to tell Chase she had been found. I licked her all over to let her know everything was going to be okay. She wrapped her arms around my neck and clung for dear life.

Deputy Sawyer fortunately knew sign language. When his mother became deaf from an ear infection, he took classes to learn how to communicate with her using his hands. He "told" Lisa that we would take her back to her parents. Chase checked her from head to toe for injuries. She had a few bruises and scrapes but otherwise seemed to be okay. Deputy Sawyer called her parents back at the camp site and gave them the good news. Chase carried her back to her very happy parents. They thanked us over and over for saving their daughter.

No problem. It's all in a day's work. Actually, I can't describe the great feeling you get when you know you have saved a life. This is the best job in the world!

The next day, Chase and I resumed house hunting. We drove and drove. We looked and looked. *Isn't it time for supper?* This house was too small, that house was too expensive. Oh well, if I couldn't eat, I'd take a nap. I curled up on the seat and began dreaming about triple cheeseburgers.

"Rocky, wake up! I've found it!" Chase exclaimed.

Yawn! What, you found my cheeseburger? I sat up and looked out the window at a very ugly house. All the windows were broken out and the paint was faded and peeling. The front porch was leaning and appeared about to collapse. This old farm house looked sad from being abandoned. It also looked strangely familiar.

Chase and I walked around the outside as he remodeled it in his mind. "Rocky, this is perfect! A little paint, a few repairs, and it will look great!"

A *little* paint and a *few* repairs? What was he thinking? The only thing this place needed was a bull dozer. Right now, the only thing I needed was supper. *Can we go?*

"I can't wait to show this place to Mom and Dad!" Chase beamed as we drove back to town.

Chase could hardly eat as he excitedly explained the potential of this old farm house to his parents. I, on the other hand, had no problem chowing down. After supper we drove back to house. When we arrived, Chase's parents just stared without saying a word.

Mrs. Carter couldn't imagine what Chase saw in this dilapidated structure and she tried to imagine the cost of making it liveable. Mr. Carter walked around and around, stroking his chin, and examining every inch.

"Well, what do you think? Isn't this great? It has large rooms, a fireplace, and five acres of land. I can finally get a horse! And look, you can see the mountains. It's centrally located between the three counties so I'll have a quick response time to rescue calls. It's perfect!"

"Chase, I don't think..." his mother started but was interrupted his father.

"I think it is almost perfect. A little hard work and you can make this a great home."

What did Chase and his father see that his mother and I did not?

"But," his mother tried to continue.

"Laura, remember our first house? It was a definite fixer-upper. With love, sweat, and a few tears, we turned it into a fine home. I think this could work out great for Chase. The price is good, the location is great, and he can remodel it just the way he wants."

"You're right, John," his mother conceded, "Chase, this can be a great house."

The next day, Chase met with the real estate agent to sign the contract. He went to the bank and secured the loan with his down payment. He went to a home improvement store and stocked the bed of his pickup with paint, lumber, nails and other items for the restoration project.

We got up early the next morning and headed to our new home. I still wasn't sure Chase had made the right decision. Oh well, a guy has to do what a guy has to do.

We arrived to find the yard filled with cars and people. Chase's friends from Trinity E.M.S., the fire department, the sheriff's office, and the police department had gathered to have an old fashioned "barn-raising". The term comes from times long ago where neighbors would come together to build barns for each other. Chase was overwhelmed by the generous offers.

Chase's mother was in the backyard. She had bought Chase a cooking grill and was making hamburgers and hot dogs for the workers. *Make mine a triple cheeseburger, hold the pickles, please!* Chase's dad and some of the firefighters were ripping old boards from the roof. Other friends were scraping off old paint from the outside. Two of the police officers were rebuilding the porch. Chase eagerly joined in.

About a month later, and many hours after work and on days off, the house was finished. You wouldn't recognize it. The roof had new wood and shingles. The old siding was replaced and painted white. The trim was blue. Matching blue shutters bordered shiny new glass window panes. Mrs. Carter placed potted flowers around the new porch. Green leafy shrubs were planted around the base of the house.

The inside was even nicer. The wood floors were refinished and restored to their original beauty and shine. The walls were cleaned and painted. Mrs. Carter hung new drapes and curtains. Chase brought his old bedroom furniture from home and bought the rest from a second-hand store. His friends gave him house-warming gifts that included new dishes, pots and pans, a toaster, a coffee maker, an even an ice cream maker. *Yum!* His parents bought a new microwave, stove, and refrigerator.

Chase hung several pictures around the house. Over the fireplace he placed our framed certificates and pictures of us at rescues. In the center was the heart of everything. His parents had framed the newspaper article with our picture and the heading, "Stray Dog Saves Boy's Life."

Chase relaxed on the couch and surveyed his new kingdom. I curled up beside him and drifted back in time. We had come so far together. He was an ornery kid always looking for trouble. I was an abandoned pup looking for a home. We were a couple of misfits looking for a purpose in life. We found each other and found our purpose. There would be many more adventures; many more rescue missions, and many more lives to save.

Beep! Beep! Beep!

That was Chase's pager. The message read, "Explosion at High School. Students injured." We rushed out and jumped into our giant 4 wheel drive rescue truck. Chase flipped the switches that turned on the flashing red and blue lights. I took my place in the passenger seat. The siren began its wail and the powerful engine roared onto the highway.

This is what we do, because a dog and a guy have to do what a dog and a guy have to do.

LaVergne, TN USA
29 June 2010
187715LV00007B/27/P